The Lost Books

THE SCROLL OF KINGS

The Lost Books

THE
SCROLL
OF
KINGS

WITHDRAWN

SARAH PRINEAS

HARPER
An Imprint of HarperCollins*Publishers*

The Lost Books: The Scroll of Kings
Copyright © 2018 by Sarah Prineas
All rights reserved. Printed in the United States of America.
No part of this book may be used or reproduced in any manner
whatsoever without written permission except in the case of brief quotations
embodied in critical articles and reviews. For information address
HarperCollins Children's Books, a division of HarperCollins Publishers,
195 Broadway, New York, NY 10007.
www.harpercollinschildrens.com

Library of Congress Control Number: 2017954075
ISBN 978-0-06-266558-4

Typography by Carla Weise
18 19 20 21 22   CG/LSCH   10 9 8 7 6 5 4 3 2 1
❖
First Edition

To my dear friend Michelle Edwards.
"Strength to your sword arm!"

... books are people
—people who have managed to stay alive
by hiding between the covers of a book.
—E. B. WHITE

The pages were bothering Alex.

The pages, of course, were the magical pieces of paper that acted as the librarian's servants. They floated around doing whatever Master Farnsworth ordered, as long as it was something simple, like "Fetch me a cup of tea," and not something complicated, like "Go alphabetize the encyclopedias."

Alex, as the librarian's assistant, or apprentice, or whatever he was, did not have pages of his own.

So when his master's pages fluttered around his head like giant anxious moths, he tried to ignore them. He had work to do. Librarian Farnsworth had ordered him to compare two alphabetized book lists. Alex had his elbows on the table and his hands gripping his hair, forcing himself to concentrate. He was on the letter *R*. Just eight letters to go, and he'd be done.

Gritting his teeth, he started on the letter *S*.

A page flitted past him.

"Go away," Alex said to it, and kept his eyes grimly on his work.

Another page floated past. Then another one.

Master Farnsworth's pages were made of paper that was wrinkled and yellowed and tattered around the edges, and one of them had been torn nearly in half and then pasted back together again so that it was sort of scarred down the middle.

The scarred page rustled, trying to get Alex's attention.

"All right, all right," he muttered. "Just a moment." Carefully he marked his place and was about to look up when the page rolled itself into a tube and bonked him on the head.

"What was *that* for?" Alex protested. It hadn't hurt, but it was annoying.

The scarred page unrolled itself. Alex saw a single word written on it in faint, almost illegible letters.

[defunct]

"What?" he asked.

Another page darted closer. A jumble of letters

stuttered across its surface and then disappeared. Then four more pages clustered around Alex, shivering. That was six total—all of Master Farnsworth's pages, as far as he knew. This was not normal behavior.

"Defunct?" Alex asked, getting to his feet. They were trying to tell him something, but the pages were simple creatures. They didn't always make sense.

The scarred page—the boldest one—floated closer. Shaky letters took shape on the yellowed paper.

[expired

overdue

off the shelf]

All of the pages were trembling, and crowding even closer. Alex felt a sudden jolt of worry. "It's all right," he tried to reassure them. "Do you want me to come with you?"

At that, the pages whirled around him, then streamed toward the door at the end of the reading room.

Feeling suddenly certain that something awful had happened, Alex followed them, hurrying between looming bookshelves until he reached the quiet corner where the librarian sometimes napped. His cot was surrounded by stacks of books. Like any proper librarian, Master Farnsworth did not fold over a corner of a page to mark his place, so his books were bristling with torn-off bits of paper used to mark where he'd stopped reading.

With the pages hovering at his shoulder, Alex stood beside the cot, looking down at his master. The old man lay with his gnarled hands holding a book that was open, facedown, on his chest.

He must have fallen asleep while reading. The librarian, being ancient, slept a good deal, and didn't move around much at the best of times. It was a shame to wake him. He looked so peaceful, lying there.

Too peaceful. Alex leaned closer. Oh, *no*. The librarian wasn't breathing.

"Master Farnsworth?" Alex went to his knees beside the cot. "Sir?" He reached out to shake the librarian's shoulder to wake him up. But his master was stiff as a board and pretty solidly dead.

He'd probably been gone for hours.

Alex swallowed several times, blinked several more times, then scrambled to his feet and stood looking sorrowfully down at the body.

The librarian had been a creature of dust and paper; a strong wind could have blown him away. He'd been skinny and bent, his face a mass of wrinkles, his hair spun-white cobwebs. To read, he peered through a pair of spectacles that had inch-thick lenses smudged with fingerprints.

Alex frowned. There was something strange.

The book rested on the librarian's chest, as if the old man had been reading it when he died. But he wasn't wearing his spectacles.

Crouching, Alex gently pulled the book from under his master's folded hands. The first thing he noticed about it was a symbol burned into the leather cover.

Below it, the title.

VINES: PLANTS OF WONDER

That was odd. As far as Alex knew, his master had no interest at all in gardening.

The second thing Alex noticed was that his master's pages had fled from the room. Or maybe, now that they'd delivered their message, they had disappeared forever. He didn't know what happened to a librarian's pages after their master had died.

He wondered why Master Farnsworth had been reading about vines. Without thinking, he flipped open the book.

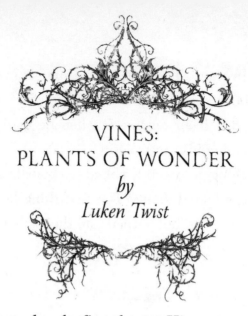

VINES:
PLANTS OF WONDER
by
Luken Twist

He turned to the first chapter. His eyes were drawn to the words at the top of the page, and he started to read.

The vine is a quite wondrous plant. It seems simple, yet it can grow at astounding speed. It can cling, twine around, climb, and in the case of some species, it can strangle.

Alex kept reading. He turned a page.

And realized that the tips of his fingers had gone numb.

And that he couldn't look away.

The numbness was spreading to his hands, which were clenched around the edges of the book. His heart pounded.

And then, the merest sliver of a pale green tendril emerged from behind the next page, which he hadn't turned yet. It quested about, almost like it was sniffing.

It was just a tiny vine, no bigger than a pea shoot.

Alex watched his own hand reach out and turn the page.

Exposed, the little vine uncoiled itself and nosed toward him. A second later, it had curled around his wrist.

"Gah!" Alex shouted. He shook the vine off his hand and dropped the book. It lay open on the dusty floor. As he watched, the tiny vine sniffed about. Then it fixed on him again. It twined from the book, growing longer and thicker, a green rope studded with shiny leaves. Like a snake, it crawled over the floor toward him.

Alex backed away, looking for anything he could use to fend it off. A second vine erupted from the book and slithered across the floor. Before he could dodge it, the first vine had wrapped itself around his ankle.

And then it was twining around his leg, and it had grown thorns, which bit into him.

With sudden horror, Alex realized what had happened to Master Farnsworth. The librarian had opened the book, started to read, and then . . .

His hands shaking, Alex ripped the vine off his leg.

Its thorns tore at his skin, and he left blood spattered around him as he stumbled back.

He had to get the book closed—or he'd end up just like his master.

The vine sniffed at the drops and then sent out little rootlets, which poked into the blood and sucked it up. Then, its strength renewed, it surged after him again.

Alex grabbed up a book from his master's reading pile and flung it at the vine. It dodged it and struck at him like a snake. The other vine was growing up the wall and sending out more tendrils that reached for him like long, green fingers.

He ducked and hurled another book as a thick, ropy, almost muscular vine reached for him. Looking wildly around, he saw the vines book lying open on the floor. At the same moment, all of the vines hissed through the air, coming after him. Fighting through the clinging tendrils, Alex lunged toward the book. He reached for it, but the vines pulled him back, dragging him over the stone floor.

He clenched his teeth. "I don't *think* so," he told the vines.

A tendril looped around his neck and tightened like strangling fingers. Black spots appeared in his vision, and he gasped for breath.

With an almighty effort, Alex lunged toward the book, grabbed it, and slammed it closed.

The vines evaporated like smoke.

Panting for breath, Alex got to his feet and stared down at the book. He rubbed his neck.

Well. That had been interesting.

He knew what a librarian was supposed to be. Master Farnsworth had been a cataloger of books—books that sat tamely on their shelves gathering dust—and a keeper of the keys that kept books safely locked up. If anyone had a question that could only be settled by looking at a book, they would go to a librarian, who would consult his or her collection and come back with an answer.

But Alex had reasons—*very* good reasons—for suspecting that librarians had once been much more than just catalogers and keepers.

And that books were much more than they seemed.

He wished he could ask his master about it.

But he couldn't. Because the librarian was dead.

The library was owned by Dowager Duchess Purslane, who was obsessed with two things.

The first thing was genealogy. The library in her castle was stuffed with tediously boring family archives, insipid family letters, and crumbling diaries written by ancestors who had been dead for three hundred years. That kind of thing.

As far as Alex was concerned, barely any of it counted as real books, and almost all of it could be burned to the ground without any loss.

The second thing was roses.

Alex found the duchess in the castle's extensive gardens, bent over a bush with pruning shears in one hand and a bunch of late-autumn blooms in the other.

"Duchess Purslane," Alex began, "I have some bad news."

The duchess was tall and rather bony, and had the rich brown skin of the old nobility. She peered short-sightedly at him over her shoulder. "Who are you?"

He gritted his teeth. "The librarian's apprentice."

She turned back to the roses. "The librarian doesn't have an apprentice." *Snip, snip, snip* went the garden shears.

"Yes he does," Alex corrected her, keeping a grip on his patience. "He did, I mean. I've been here for months."

More snipping. "Well, what do you want, boy?" She cast him a frowning glance, from the top of his dusty blond head, to his inky fingers and shabby clothes, to the tips of his worn shoes. "Bad news, I think you said?"

"Yes." Alex nodded. "The librarian is dead."

The dowager duchess straightened and blinked rapidly. A hand went to her chest. "Oh dear. Dead, you say?"

"Yes," Alex answered. "He was very old, as you know." Before she could comment, he went on. "He trained me well." That was a complete lie, but she'd never know it. "I'll take over as head librarian. I can begin immediately and set things to rights."

"Wait a moment," the duchess said slowly. "Now I remember you."

Oh, blast it, Alex thought. Into a million tiny pieces.

The duchess pointed at him with the pruning shears. "You're the one who wanted to destroy my library."

"Not *destroy*," Alex insisted.

"Destroy," repeated the duchess. "You wanted to throw away the castle records!"

"Not all of them," Alex said. "Just the useless things. After all, who needs copies of two-hundred-year-old laundry lists? Or," he added, because he couldn't help it, "a crumbling diary written by a soldier stationed at an outpost where nothing happens for *twenty years*?"

"That soldier was my great-grandmother's second cousin once removed!" exclaimed the dowager duchess.

"Twenty years of *It was foggy today*," Alex scoffed.

"The sergeant-at-arms got drunk again. Chicken stew for dinner. Why even bother with it?"

The dowager duchess gasped. *"Why . . . even . . ."*

Relentlessly, Alex went on. "Papers like that don't belong in a library. You might as well use them for wrapping up fish guts in the kitchen. Or for lining a birdcage. Or in the privy."

"You dare suggest such a use for my family papers! You horrible, horrible boy!" She waved her roses in the direction of the castle, scattering petals around them both. "Out!"

"What?" Alex asked blankly. "You can't throw me out. You've got a problem in your library. A big one."

"You!" cried the dowager duchess. "The problem is *you.*"

"No, wait," Alex protested. "Something snaky is going on in there. You need a librarian to deal with it."

"Then I will get one." The duchess brandished the pruning shears, and Alex stepped quickly back to avoid getting poked. "But not you. Get out. Pack your things and get out of my castle. You are no librarian, and you will never set foot in my library again!"

2

"*No librarian*," Alex grumbled to himself. "What does *she* know about it?"

He was in a hurry. When he'd started back toward the castle library, the dowager duchess had gone in the other direction, and he knew where she was headed— to get her castle steward to toss him out the front gate.

But there was something he needed to do before he let that happen. It wasn't *pack his things*, either. He didn't have any *things*.

What he did have was plans.

Almost four months ago, when he'd convinced the librarian to take him on as an apprentice, he'd had good reasons for coming to Purslane Castle.

For one thing, anybody who might possibly be searching for him would never think of looking for him here. He was as good as dead and buried in the dowager duchess's moldering, rose-encrusted castle.

For another thing, he'd suspected that Farnsworth, being ancient, knew secret librarian things and could answer some questions. Questions that had been eating away at Alex the way a biscuit beetle nibbled through the pages of an infested book.

One day he and the librarian had been drinking their weekly cup of tea together, after which the old man would show Alex things, like how to restitch a binding, or stop the damp from making a book turn moldy. These were important things for a librarian to know, but Alex was curious about something else.

"Sir," he'd asked, when the librarian had finished showing off forty-two different kinds of frass.

Frass was bug droppings. By looking at what frass was left behind, you could tell what kinds of bugs were infesting the books in a library. Definitely not what he really needed to know.

"Master Farnsworth," Alex had asked, "is there something strange about books?"

The librarian had been examining a little bottle of frass from a biscuit beetle. Deliberately, he'd slotted the bottle back into the box that contained forty-one other tiny jars of frass, all labeled in the librarian's spidery script. Then Merwyn Farnsworth stroked his beard. When he spoke, he had a high voice, birdlike. "Books, strange? No. Certainly not. What an odd question to ask, ah . . . uh . . . boy."

As usual, he'd forgotten Alex's name.

"Not just strange," Alex had persisted. "This is serious. Books are . . . they're not just books, are they?"

The old man had shaken his head. "Books are not books? Whatever are you talking about?"

But he'd had a gleam in his eye when he'd said it. So Alex pushed. "You know," he'd insisted. "Librarians keep books locked up and hidden away. There must be a reason for that. You know their secrets."

"The only thing books do," the old man had said, shaking his head, "is gather dust. Speaking of which, you'd better dust the duchess's collection of her great-uncle's letters."

But Alex felt certain that his master knew a lot more than he was telling. Because at the very center of the castle library, he'd found a door to a room.

The door was made of thick ironwood. Banded with metal. Doorknob in the middle, and under it, a keyhole. It was pretty much impenetrable.

Something was in there, Alex knew it. Some kind of dangerous book.

Merwyn Farnsworth had the only key, and he'd kept it on a chain around his neck. Alex had asked him a thousand times to let him into the locked room.

Just to do some dusting, Alex would say. *I won't even look into the books.* A total lie, that. The very second he got in there he would have pounced on them.

But it didn't matter, because Master Farnsworth had just shaken his old, white head and put a knobbled hand over his chest, where the iron key to the room hung on its chain.

Well, Alex would get into it now.

He hurried into the castle library, and made his way to the remote corner where the librarian's body lay.

He stood, surveying the small, dusty space, looking for the book called *Vines: Plants of Wonder.* Nobody, he was absolutely certain, had come into the room while he'd been telling the duchess about the librarian's death, but the vines book was gone. Blast it, he'd missed his chance to examine it more carefully. There had been that odd symbol burned into its cover.

Alex knelt next to the cot.

"Sorry, sir," he said, then pushed aside the old man's wispy beard and felt around his neck for the chain that held the key.

It wasn't there.

Alex sat back on his heels.

Had the key been left in the door?

Possibly.

Getting to his feet, aware of the passage of time, Alex hurried to the locked room. But the key was not there, either. Alex twisted the knob in the middle of the door, but it didn't turn.

Maybe the librarian had left the key in his desk.

Alex made his way through the corridors again, knowing the steward would be along shortly to deal with the librarian's body, and to kick him out of the castle for good.

The librarian's desk was just as untidy as the library.

It bothered Alex. Like an itch. A librarian needed to keep things in order, not all jumbled on the shelves. Maybe the librarian had been too old. He'd been so obsessed with bug droppings that he'd let the books get away from him.

The desk was in a poorly lit corner near the main door of the library. Keeping an eye on the door, Alex began searching the desk for the key.

There was no method to any of it. Papers were piled a foot deep, along with books, pens, dried-up bottles of ink, scraps of paper with illegible writing, and enough dust to choke a camel. At the back of the desk were rows of cubbyholes that held nubs of pencils, balls of twine, a nose-hair clipper, and plenty of dead spiders.

With a growing sense that he needed to hurry, Alex went through all of it.

No key.

"Blast it," he said, sitting back.

His eyes fell on the in-box, almost buried by papers at the edge of the desk. It was a hinged box where the librarian kept all of his letters. The librarian hadn't gotten many letters, but he had answered them all. Eventually.

Lifting the lid, Alex found that the box was almost empty.

The single envelope had been sealed with a thick blob of black wax with some sort of seal stamped into it. The paper was creamy and thick. Expensive, Alex thought. He rubbed it between his fingers. He was sure it was from the paper-makers at Barrettim. The finest paper available anywhere.

He pulled out a two-page letter. The top edge of the paper was gilded. Below that was a crest that he recognized, a bear holding a garden spade in one paw, a sword in the other, in black with accents in gold.

The royal crest. Black for the rich dirt of the Kingdom of Aethel, gold for ripened wheat. He wasn't sure what the bear had to do with anything.

Alex checked the second page to see the signature.

The letter was from the queen!

Before he could start reading it, there was a bustle at the door of the library, and it was suddenly flung open.

In the doorway stood the Purslane Castle steward, with one of the stable grooms at his back.

Jumping to his feet, Alex shoved the royally crested paper and envelope into his jacket pocket. He'd had a run-in with the steward before, when he'd searched the castle, trying to find an extra key to the locked library room. The steward didn't like Alex. The feeling was decidedly mutual.

In the doorway, the steward's beady eyes darted from bookshelves, to dark corners, to the desk. Like any normal person, he was reluctant to enter a library. "Well," he complained, "where is he?"

Alex felt a pang of sorrow. Merwyn Farnsworth had not only refused to reveal any librarian secrets, he'd refused to admit that there even *were* secrets. Mostly he'd known way too much about bug poop. But the old man was rather unexpectedly dead, and that was a sad thing. "In the back," Alex said, pointing.

The steward scuffed through some scattered papers. "Are Farnsworth's magic page thingies lurking about?"

Alex shook his head. "They've disappeared."

"And what about you?" the steward asked, eyeing Alex. "You don't have any of those pages, do you?"

"No," Alex had to admit.

"Good." The steward shoved aside a tottering pile of papers and came farther into the library.

Alex knew that most of the duchess's papers were worthless, but still it made him cringe. "Careful," he warned.

The steward paused, then turned. "Careful, is it?" He folded his burly arms. "Jock, come here." He summoned the hulking groom from the doorway, then pointed at Alex. "Duchess's orders. Toss this annoying scrap out the front gate. Give him a good kick, while you're at it, to send him on his way."

"Will do," said the groom, and grinned widely, exposing a missing front tooth. "Come along, you." With a long arm, he reached out and grabbed Alex's shoulder.

"Kick me and you'll regret it," Alex threatened.

"Oh sure." The groom shoved him toward the library door. "Let's go."

As Alex stumbled out into the hallway, he bumped straight into the duchess, who had two more servants with her. "Make sure he hasn't stolen anything," she ordered.

"There's nothing in your library worth stealing," Alex shot back.

The duchess's face turned dusky red, and she made a gabbling noise like a chicken. "Throw him out!" she managed to say, pointing at the stairway that led down to the main part of the castle.

The groom grabbed Alex by the collar of his jacket. "Come along, annoying scrap," he said cheerfully, and dragged him away.

The castle was built on traditional lines, with a main gate through six-foot-thick walls and a drawbridge that was never closed, leading over a moat filled with muck and dead leaves. When the groom reached the road on the other side of the bridge, he planted a heavy foot in the middle of Alex's back and gave a mighty shove.

Alex stumbled forward, tripped, and landed with a *splut* on a pile of horse dung, right in the middle of the road. Sitting up, he shot the groom a venomous look, and spat dust out of his mouth.

"And stay out!" the groom yelled.

Climbing to his feet, Alex turned away, just so he wouldn't have to see the groom's grinning face. Fine. He was going.

Then he thought better of it. He turned back. The

groom was still standing on the drawbridge, arms folded. Behind him, the castle loomed. Thorny rose vines grew up the towers and spilled over the castle walls.

"Hey, Jock," Alex called.

"You're not coming back in," the groom answered. "So don't even bother asking."

"Yeah, I know." Alex glanced at the sky. Late afternoon—almost evening. He needed to be getting along. But first he had to warn them. With his chin, he pointed at the rose-encrusted castle. "Tell them if they find the key to the room in the middle of the library, they shouldn't open it unless they've got a librarian or two with them who knows what they're doing."

Jock rolled his eyes. "Key. Room. Right."

"Right," Alex repeated. "And if they find a book about vines, they absolutely must not read it."

Jock pretended to yawn.

"It's important," Alex warned him.

"Oh, sure it is," the groom said. "Now quit stalling. Get going."

"Idiot," Alex muttered under his breath. But he couldn't go yet. He had to lay a false trail. "Listen, if anybody comes looking for me, tell them I'm heading . . ." He paused and looked around, then chose a direction at random. ". . . west. Toward the border. I'm going to get a ship to go to Xan to study in the great libraries there. All right?"

The groom shrugged. "Sure. What name?"

"Alex," he replied. "Alexandren."

"Right. Traveling west. Now off you go."

Turning his back on the castle, Alex headed out.

He wasn't sure where he was going, but he knew one thing for sure. It wouldn't be west. It would be anywhere but west.

3

One bitterly cold winter day when he was ten years old, Alex had hidden in his father's library.

It was a fairly large library, but even so, like most people, his father was not a reader. Far from it. Books were useful for starting fires, his pa thought, if you ripped the pages out first, and for propping up tables with one leg too short. His library was kept locked because there was no librarian, and the untended books were left to grow moldy.

But young Alex had found the key, and he took refuge there. It was quiet. There were no men-at-arms or women-at-arms in the library. No sword practice. No strategy and tactics, no military history lessons.

And there were books.

He had made his own place, a cozy nest hidden behind a curtain in a windowed recess. There he kept a stack of books that he read like a thousand grasshoppers eating their way through a wheat field. By the time he was twelve, he'd read every book in his father's library. Twice.

Everybody knew how to read, of course, but for practical reasons. Not for reading *books*, of all things. Librarians were so obsessive about keeping their libraries locked up all the time that books had come to be treated with suspicion. There were no new books, only old ones. Most people felt a little creepy about going into a library. Even so, as far as Alex knew, books were inanimate objects that sat on the shelf getting dusty, unless he read them, in which case the dust got on him.

But one day he found a book on a top shelf that, somehow, he'd overlooked. Standing on a chair, on tiptoe, he pulled it out from where it was hiding behind a rack of encyclopedias. The book was very thick, and had a worn red leather cover and no title. It smelled of smoke and cinnamon spice. It was much heavier than it looked. Alex heaved it off the shelf and took it to his lair, where he wrapped himself in a blanket. Opening the book, he started to read.

And the world around him went away. There was

no itchy wool blanket, no chill seeping up from the stone floor, no ache in his bones from sword practice the day before. There was just the book. Even the feel of the bumpy cover faded away, and so did the faintly smoky smell wafting up from the pages.

The book had him in its clutches.

And then, as he read, the black words spooling across the creamy white page, the letters had twitched, pulled themselves up, and marched across the paper and up his ice-cold fingers. He'd watched, fascinated, feeling prickly all over as the words crawled like spiky black ants over the back of his hand, then encircled his left wrist. The letters shifted, blurring into one word, then another.

BOOK, he read, then **STOLEN** and **THE** and **NEVER**. Then a strange word, **CODEX**. Then the letters shifted again, jumbling into nonsense.

As Alex wondered what a *codex* was, the library door had slammed open with an echoing *bang*. A moment later, two of his father's soldiers ripped the curtain away from his hiding place. He had a moment to blink owlishly up at them before they grabbed him.

"So here's where you've been hiding, kid!" exclaimed Jeffen, who was one of the Family, his father's most trusted soldiers. Like all of the Family, Jeffen was sort of like an older sibling to Alex. An extremely loud, obnoxious, annoying, teasing, redheaded big brother who also happened to be an expert swordsman. Jeffen had looked uneasily around the dim, dusty library. "Kind of snaky in here, isn't it?"

Alex had given him his most dire scowl. "Go away."

"Can't," Jeffen said with a cheerful shrug. "Your pa wants you."

The other Family soldier was a woman-at-arms, Franciss. "You know what they say, Alex," she said. "'Children should be seen and not hide.'"

"That is not what they say," Alex had snapped, "and I'm not hiding. I've been *reading.*" The words that had crawled onto his skin started prickling like lots of tiny needles. The prickling feeling became an almost unbearable stinging, and the letters flowed over his own hands and spilled out of the book he was holding, onto the floor, and then swarmed over Jeffen and Franciss. The words slithered up the legs of their trousers and up their sleeves.

Jeffen had shrieked and ripped open his uniform. "Gah!" he shouted as he pulled it off and flung it to the floor, and then started stamping on it. At the same time, Franciss drew her sword and spun in circles, looking for something to fight. A word crawled out

-27-

from under her collar and up her neck, and her eyes bulged with fright.

"Franciss, put your sword away," Alex said, using the sharp tone his pa used when giving orders, "before you skewer somebody." Then he turned to Jeffen. "And quit yelling about *ants all over you.*" Somehow, he'd known exactly what to do next. Pointing at the words, he shouted one of the markings that had been printed on his wrist: "Codex!"

And the words had peeled off of Franciss's neck, and off of Jeffen's arms, and flown through the air toward him.

"Codex!" he ordered again, opening the red-leather-covered book, and he'd felt certain the words would obey him—and they did, flowing back to him. He snapped the book closed.

But a few words had stayed behind.

Black spots flickered in his vision, and his skin felt prickly all over. Then his eyes cleared and he saw black letters printed around the pale skin of his left wrist, like a tattoo, or a bracelet. The words didn't spell anything, or at least they didn't make any sense when he tried to read them. But he'd been marked, and he had suddenly known with a fierce certainty that this meant he wasn't supposed to be a soldier like his pa.

No. He was a librarian.

There were three problems, that he knew of, with this fact.

The first problem was that every librarian that he'd ever met—and he'd met a few since leaving home—was ancient. None of them would teach him anything. None of them would tell him any of their librarian secrets—and he *knew* they had secrets.

The second problem was that every true librarian had pages—magical pieces of paper that carried out the librarian's orders. Unfortunately, Alex didn't have even one page to help him.

The third problem was the biggest. His father. Pa valued swords, not words. According to him, librarians were *useless* and *spineless* and basically *less* in every way.

And yet.

Alex had, of course, told his father about the book that had gone after the Family soldiers. Or the *Red Codex*, as he thought of it.

"It wasn't a book," Jeffen said scornfully. "It was ants. That library is infested."

"It was not ants," Alex insisted. "They were words. Words that crawled out of a book."

"You know what they say," Franciss had put in. "'You can't judge a book by the color of its spots.'"

"*Nobody* says that, Franciss," Alex had said with a glare.

"I say it," Franciss argued. She appealed to Jeffen. "Didn't I just say it?"

"All right now," Pa had interrupted just as Alex was about to explode with annoyance. His father had just come in from sword practice. He was huge in his leather armor, with the broadsword strapped across his back. "What was this book about, son?"

Alex had opened his mouth to answer, when he realized that he couldn't remember a single word of what he'd read. "It's . . . it's about the history of . . . of making swords," he'd told his pa. He hadn't been a very good liar when he was younger. He'd gotten better since then.

"Show me this book, then," his pa had said.

Alex went to fetch it, but the Red Codex was nowhere to be found.

"See?" Jeffen said, when Alex came back empty-handed. "Ants."

Ants or not, that was enough for Alex's pa to decide that they needed a proper librarian.

Alex had told him that he wanted to do it.

Pa had snorted. "Why waste your time?" he'd asked.

And then Alex had told Pa that he wasn't going to study the sword anymore, or military tactics, or strategy, or any of the things that Pa thought were important. He showed him the bracelet of letters printed around his wrist and said that he was going to be a librarian.

And his father had laughed. "You, a librarian?" he had boomed. "Hah. My only son will not be wasting his life looking after a bunch of moldy books."

Alex had argued and shouted and had even tried to reason with him, but Pa wouldn't listen. Instead he'd brought in a professional, an old woman librarian with two faded-looking pages who refused to teach Alex anything.

He had tried telling her about the Red Codex.

When he'd told her that the words had crawled off the page and onto his skin, her eyes had gone wide. When he'd told her how he had ordered the words back into the book again, she had given him a sour, suspicious look and called him a liar. When he'd asked her what the word *codex* meant, exactly, she went to his father. Then she locked the library and wouldn't let Alex back into it. Pa's orders.

The betrayal of it still hurt.

Because no matter what his pa said, no matter that he didn't have his own pages to act as his servants, and even though all the other librarians he'd met were dusty and decrepit and secretive, Alex knew exactly what he was meant to be.

He just wasn't sure how he was supposed to *do* it.

With his own eyes, he had seen books that did *not*

just sit on shelves getting dusty—first the Red Codex in his pa's library, and then the book at Purslane that had attacked him with vines and had probably killed Merwyn Farnsworth. Clearly librarians were more than just keepers of the keys to library doors. There was something magical about books, something dangerous, something more. But what *more*, exactly, he didn't know.

Well, he'd just have to figure it out as he went along.

He was sure about one thing, at least. He couldn't go back home, even though he missed . . . certain people. He had to go on. He had to prove himself, somehow.

Down the road a short distance from Purslane Castle was the town of Purslane, which sat on a crossroads. There was an inn on its busiest corner, which was not particularly busy, because people didn't travel much these days.

Alex's stomach growled. He looked down at himself. He was dusty and disheveled and . . .

Blast. There was a smear of horse dung across the front of his jacket. He tried brushing it off and ended up with horse dung all over his hands. Giving a shrug, he wiped his hands on his jacket and headed toward the center of Purslane, passing shops and people and wagons loaded with wheat and vegetables grown in the farmland that encircled the town. The weeklong harvest festival had just ended, and everyone was busy putting their gardens to bed, and storing food for the winter. A few people glanced at him. It wasn't usual to see strangers in a little town like Purslane. Most people, Alex had realized after he left home, never went farther than five miles from the place where they'd been born. Even so, as far as the townspeople could see, he was just a scruffy-looking kid.

Little did they know, Alex thought darkly to himself.

He spared one last glance at the castle behind him. He hated leaving that locked room and its potential dangers. He'd tried to warn them, but he knew the duchess and the steward had not taken him seriously. And he hated leaving behind the four books he'd been reading. A book half read was a bother. Like a toothache. It niggled.

There was nothing he could do about it now.

As he stood there, he felt another wash of sorrow that Merwyn Farnsworth was dead. The old man had kept his secrets, and he'd been a little weird about bugs, but he had been kind to Alex.

On Alex's left wrist, the bracelet of letters itched, as it often did. He glanced down at them. Then he blinked and looked more closely. For the first time since the Red Codex had marked him, the letters were shifting, climbing over each other, rejumbling into a new order. For just a moment, a word formed.

GO

Then the letters shifted back into a jumble again.

All right, *that* was snaky. "I'm going," Alex said to the letters.

But they didn't spell anything back to him. With a shrug, he went on.

When he arrived at the Purslane Inn, he had a bit of luck. Going through the front door, he found an unattended counter. On it rested a paper where guests could sign in; next to it was a pot of ink with a cap on it, and a metal-nibbed pen. With a quick look around, Alex pulled out the letter he'd stolen from the librarian's desk; it had a second page with half a blank page under the queen's signature. He tore the paper, taking the blank half and stuffing the rest of it into his pocket. Dipping the pen into the ink, he wrote a quick note, using the dowager duchess's handwriting, which he had made a point of studying during his time at the castle.

To the Inn at Purslane—

To the bearer of this note provide all finest accoutrements, bed, dinner, breakfast, and supplies to see him on the road tomorrow. Send the bill to me at the castle.

Signed,

Dowager Duchess Purslane

There. That should do it.

No sooner had he set down the pen than the innkeeper, a stout woman with fiery red hair, bustled into the room, wiping her hands on a stained apron.

"Well, what d'you want?" she asked impatiently.

Alex took a quick glance at the note he'd just written. The ink was still wet. Surreptitiously, he waved it, trying to get it dry before he had to hand it over. "I'll take a room for the night," he said, "and the best dinner you've got."

"Hmm." The innkeeper eyed him.

Alex knew he looked a little rough around the edges, but he eyed her right back.

"And you've got money to pay for this best room and fine dinner?" she asked dubiously.

"Even better," Alex told her, and held out the note, which hopefully wouldn't smear when she took it.

The innkeeper cocked her head and squinted down

at the paper. "From the duchess." She read on, muttering to herself. "Ack-coo-tree-monts, is it? Hmm. That's the duchess's signature, though. I suppose this seems in order." She glanced up at him, and gave a suspicious sniff. "What's that I smell?"

"Yes, I smell like horse," Alex said. "That's because I'm a groom in the duchess's stable." He took off the stinky jacket. "I'll need you to wash this for me."

The innkeeper stared at him.

"Accoutrements," Alex told her, putting into his voice every bit of confidence he had, every bit of *I am on a special mission for the duchess and how dare you doubt me?*

The innkeeper blinked and then, slowly, she reached out and took the jacket, and Alex knew he'd won.

"Have it ready for me by tomorrow morning," he said. "Along with the supplies the duchess mentioned in her note. I'll go into the dining room to wait for dinner."

With that, he breezed past her into the large common area. Finding a small table next to the inn's row of front windows, he sat down and let out a relieved breath. The duchess, he guessed, would pay for his stay at the inn when the innkeeper sent her the bill. She wouldn't be happy about it—rather, she'd be furious—but it couldn't be helped, and she owed him that much, anyway, for almost four months of work.

A waiter, a red-haired kid who had to be the innkeeper's son, appeared and took his order for the finest dinner they had.

"Where you headed?" the kid asked.

None of your business, Alex thought. But the men-at-arms who might, possibly, come looking for him would ask at an inn like this, so he'd better lay his false trail from here, too. He told the redheaded kid the same lie about heading west to the border and taking a ship to Xan.

"Uh-huh," the kid said, looking bored.

"And my name is Alexandren, in case anybody comes here asking about me."

The kid shrugged. As soon as he'd gone, Alex pulled out the letter he'd taken from the librarian's desk—it was rather crumpled now, and the second page was torn in half, but the gilt edging was as shiny as ever.

He'd seen the queen's signature on the second page. The date at the top indicated that it had been sent less than two weeks ago. Eagerly, Alex started reading from the beginning.

Librarian Merwyn Farnsworth
Purslane Castle
Extershire
Aethel

Librarian Farnsworth,

It is with sadness that we report to you the death of Maeviss Clark, who had served us as Royal Librarian. She made it known that you, Librarian Farnsworth, were next in eminence to her, and should be appointed in her place, should anything happen to her.

As you may know, the Royal Library, housed in the Winter Palace, is extensive, consisting of many rooms and innumerable books, texts, codices, scrolls, maps, diaries, tomes, and handwritten manuscripts. Certain parts of the collection may have not been properly cataloged in many years.

In order to put the books into better order, and to guard them well, you are required to journey to Aethel's Winter Palace to take up the position of Royal Librarian. Upon arrival, report to the Royal Steward, who will direct you further.

We request that you make all haste to take up this position.

By order of the Queen, Kenneret the Third

Q. Kenneret III

Another librarian, dead.

Quite a coincidence, Alex thought.

As far as he knew, the queen, who hadn't been queen for very long, had never met Merwyn Farnsworth. She hadn't even written the letter; that had been done, he guessed, by a secretary, or this steward person that was mentioned, and the queen had just added her signature at the end.

The queen wanted Merwyn Farnsworth to report to the palace?

Well, Alex thought, this was his chance. He would **GO**. If the queen needed a librarian, she was going to get one.

4

I must have added wrong, Queen Kenneret thought to herself. She looked over the column of numbers that had been submitted to her by the royal steward, who was responsible for . . . well, basically for overseeing everything in the Winter Palace. House-keeping, hiring the servants, putting together the budgets, ordering supplies, and so on. The steward stood at attention four paces from her desk. As always, Dorriss had not a gray hair out of place. She wore the uniform of the royal servants, a dress made of black silk with the kingdom's seal, the bear, sword, and spade, embroidered in gold on her sleeve. At her waist she wore a belt, and hanging from it was a chatelaine, a chain with a ring of keys at its end that jingled every time she took a step. Behind the steward stood two footmen, wearing gold-and-black-striped waistcoats, and two secretaries holding files stuffed with important papers.

"Carry the one," Kenneret muttered, totting up the numbers again. "Nineteen, and twenty." Setting down the pencil, she sat back from her desk. "Twenty thousand. It costs twenty thousand golds to heat the Winter Palace every year." She allowed herself a brief moment of despair. Her uncle, Patchedren, would make an issue of the cost. Her uncle had been her regent until three months ago, when Kenneret had turned sixteen, which was old enough to rule the kingdom herself, he'd said. He often made issues of things, which wouldn't be so bad, except that his issues too often made her seem thoughtless or weak.

Well, there was nothing else to be done—they would simply have to stop heating parts of the palace, even though the harvest festival was over and nobles and courtiers from all over the kingdom had started descending on the palace to spend the winter doing what nobles and courtiers did. Namely feasting, gossiping, carrying on secret intrigues, and challenging each other to duels. Why couldn't they all just stay home until spring?

Ugh, and her bottom hurt from sitting on this uncomfortable velvet chair for the past four hours. And her crown—the simple gold circlet, for daily use—was giving her a headache.

When she opened her eyes, the steward was bowing deeply. "The numbers don't lie, Your Majesty," she said formally.

Kenneret straightened. She let her usual mask of imperturbability settle over her face. "Of course they don't," she said coolly. "For the good of the people—" It was always best to begin her proclamations that way. "For the good of the people, we authorize a reduction in the heating expenditure for the palace." Standing, she leaned over the wide, polished expanse of her desk and handed over the papers she'd been studying.

"Yes, Your Majesty," the steward said.

"We will start a fashion this winter for wearing wool and furs," Kenneret said, using the royal *we* that made her every pronouncement seem too formal. "So our courtiers don't get cold."

"Very good, Your Majesty," Dorriss said, and turned to hand the papers to one of the secretaries.

With a sigh, Kenneret sat down on her sore bottom. She was *queen*. Surely she could get a better pillow for her chair. But she did not squirm. Her back didn't even touch the chair—that's how straight she sat. "Will that be all, then, Steward?" she asked.

"There are two more things, Your Majesty," Dorriss said, turning away from the servants. "Yes, you may go," she said to the two secretaries, who, after bowing deeply, received a nod of dismissal from the queen. Dorriss pulled a letter from the file of papers she held, and scanned it. "This, Your Majesty, is from the military school at Starkcliffe. They are expelling your brother." She glanced up. "Again."

Kenneret stifled a groan. Her brother, Charleren, younger than her by a year, was far, far more trouble than he was worth. The school had kicked him out before—and they'd taken him back because she had insisted. After all, she *was* queen. "When does he arrive?" she asked, forcing her voice to remain calm.

"In a few days, Your Majesty," Dorriss answered, after scanning the letter again.

"Very well." Carefully, Kenneret placed the tips of her fingers along the edge of the shiny surface of her desk. She made herself notice the swirls in the polished wood, its deep honey color. Details. They were important. They kept her grounded, steady, even when she wanted to rip off her crown and run screaming with exasperation from the palace. She took a long, steadying breath. "We believe you said there were two more things requiring our attention?" she asked.

"Ah, yes, Your Majesty," Steward Dorriss answered. "It is about the new royal librarian, who has just arrived. I think . . ." Her lips pursed. "It may be best if Your Majesty meets him."

Kenneret sighed. She wasn't getting out of this chair anytime soon. "Very well." A library was a burden. Like an ancient, sickly maiden aunt, of little interest to anyone, but it did need a keeper.

Dorriss turned to give orders to one of the footmen to fetch the new royal librarian.

"What is his name again?" Kenneret asked.

"Farnsworth, Your Majesty," Dorriss answered, her face carefully blank. At the sound of footsteps in the hallway, she turned. "Ah, here he is."

The librarian entered her office. Kenneret blinked and tried not to stare. He was not at *all* what she had expected. He was young, for one thing, even younger than she was by at least a year, she guessed. The same age as her brother. Tall, though. Pale-skinned, with badly cut blond hair, a long nose, wearing a shirt that had once been white, with a shapeless brown jacket over it, and trousers that were a little too short, as if he'd grown taller since he was given them.

"Your Majesty," Dorriss said, her voice uninflected, "may I present Librarian Merwyn . . . ah . . . Farnsworth, most recently librarian to the Dowager

Duchess of Purslane Castle in Extershire."

Now was when he should bow. But he didn't. He just regarded her levelly, with narrowed gray eyes.

She stared back at him and felt an instant antipathy. Who did he think he *was*, not even bowing to the queen? "*You* are Merwyn Farnsworth?"

He flinched just the slightest bit as she said the name. She noticed such things—she had to, because people never *ever* told a queen what they were really thinking. He didn't like his name, she guessed. Or . . . it wasn't his name at all.

"Yes, I'm Farnsworth," he answered. "Not Merwyn, if you don't mind. Alex. I go by my middle name, Alexandren."

"We are pleased to welcome you to the Aethel Winter Palace, Librarian Farnsworth," she said formally.

"Thanks," he answered. He glanced aside at the steward. "What happened to the previous librarian?" he asked.

"She died," Dorriss answered.

"Yeah, I got that," the boy said impatiently. "It was in the letter. But *how* did she die?"

"Of old age, I believe," Dorriss said. It was, after all, her job to know such things.

"She just fell asleep one day and didn't wake up?" he asked. "Is that it?"

"That is," Dorriss said dryly, "in fact, it."

The boy looked intent. "Was she holding a book when it happened?"

Dorriss frowned ever so slightly at the question. "I do not know."

"Huh," the boy said, and absently rubbed his left wrist.

There was a moment of silence.

"Do you have the letter that we sent you?" Kenneret asked, trying to get a better sense of who he was. "The one inviting you to serve us as the royal librarian?"

"*We?*" he asked abruptly. "What *we*? What *us*?"

Kenneret caught her steward's eye. At her nod, Dorriss answered for her. "Her Majesty uses the royal *we*. It is a reminder that Her Majesty, the queen, speaks not just for herself, but for the crown and, indeed, for the kingdom."

To Kenneret's surprise, the boy nodded seriously. "Right. I get it." And then he gave her that level, searching look again, as if he was trying to see past the *we* to *I*. To her.

She didn't like it. "The letter?" she prompted.

The boy pulled a crumpled paper from the pocket of his rather ragged jacket and held it out to her, stepping closer so he could reach across the desk.

As she took it, she noticed that he had some sort of tattoo around his wrist, but even stranger, his fingers were calloused. *And,* he had lines of scars, faded to white, across the backs of his knuckles. She knew scars like that—her brother had them, too. People got them from training with the sword. Not just blunted practice swords, but real ones, with sharp edges.

What kind of librarian had advanced sword training?

She glanced at the paper, and indeed, it was the letter her steward had sent to Castle Purslane requiring Merwyn Farnsworth to take up the position of royal librarian. She tapped the edge of the paper against the polished surface of her desk. "So . . . you are a librarian," she said.

"Yes," he answered.

"Yes, *Your Majesty,*" Dorriss said pointedly. "That is the proper form of address when speaking to the queen."

He frowned, hesitated, and then said, "Yes, *Your Majesty.*"

"What, in your opinion," Kenneret asked, "is a librarian's duty?"

"Librarians look after libraries," he answered. And then added, "Your Majesty."

"And what does that involve?" she asked.

He shrugged. "Cataloging the books. Keeping the books locked up."

"That does not sound particularly interesting," she murmured, still tapping the letter on her desk, because she could see quite clearly that it annoyed him. "It seems to us, Merwyn Alexandren Farnsworth, that you are more suited to being a swordsman than a librarian."

He gave her an inimical look. "You have no idea what you're talking about."

"*Your Majesty*," reminded Dorriss softly.

"Libraries are dangerous," he went on as if Dorriss had not spoken. "*Books* are dangerous. A book is more dangerous than any sword."

Interested, Kenneret leaned closer. "And a librarian is more brave than any soldier?"

"That's right," he answered promptly, as if he'd had this argument before.

Hmm. She suspected he was being purposely over-dramatic about books—which were strange, yes, but not actually *dangerous*—so that she'd give him the job. And she didn't believe for a second that he was who he claimed to be. He was too young, too scruffy, too obnoxious. Still, he sounded educated, despite his northern accent, and she did need somebody to keep the books in order, or at least dusted, until her steward found somebody more appropriate.

"We will give you a chance to prove yourself," she said. "Until the end of the month."

"What?" he protested. "I'll barely have time to survey the shelves. Six months. A year would be better."

"End of." Kenneret smiled coolly. "The month."

"Fine," he snapped. "I'd better get started, then." And he spun on his heel and stalked out of her office. The door slammed behind him. Then it opened, and he stuck his head back into the room. "*Your Majesty*," he added, his voice etched with acid, and then slammed the door as he left again.

"My goodness," Dorriss murmured, gazing at the closed door with her eyebrows raised. "That one is going to be trouble." Then she glided closer to the desk and picked up the crumpled letter that had been sent to Merwyn Farnsworth.

With a sigh of relief, Kenneret stood up from her uncomfortable velvet chair. Before Dorriss could leave, she asked the question that had been bothering her since the beginning of the interview. "Steward, he asked about the previous librarian. There was nothing odd about her death, was there?"

"I believe not, Your Majesty," she said, adding the letter to a folder stuffed with other papers. "Does Her Majesty wish me to begin searching for someone more qualified to serve as royal librarian?"

Kenneret sighed. "Yes. We suppose that you must." She didn't think Merwyn Farnsworth—or whoever he was—could do *too* much damage to the royal library before they found somebody to replace him.

And then, with an effort, she dismissed the new librarian from her thoughts. It was only the library, after all. It was only books. She had much more important things to worry about.

5

Alex could still hear the echo of the door he'd slammed, the one that led into the queen's office. Storming out of there had probably been a mistake, but when she'd said he had until the end of the month—fifteen days!—to set the royal library to rights, it had infuriated him beyond all toleration. A whole team of expertly trained librarians couldn't do it. He certainly couldn't, not all by himself.

Still, he'd started on this road, and he couldn't stop now. He had to keep going and see what happened, even though he'd probably wind up either tossed out the front gate of the palace, or tracked down by the people he'd been trying to avoid for the past few months, or, most likely, he'd fail so spectacularly that *blast it into a million pieces* would no longer be just a figure of speech.

Alex stalked down the long hallway, walking fast until he'd taken the edge off of his annoyance. The queen obviously didn't believe for a second that he was a librarian. There she'd sat, a smug smile on her face, all stiffly formal in her lacy brocade dress, with a heavy-looking gold circlet resting on her intricately braided brown hair and stacks of jeweled rings on every finger. Still, she was young, not that much older than he was, and she'd seemed uncomfortable. All that *royal we* and *Your Majesty* business, as if she had to be constantly reminded that yes, she was the queen. Or maybe she had to constantly remind everybody else. He wondered who had her doubting herself so badly.

Never mind the queen. He had more important things to deal with.

The library had to be around here somewhere.

He kept going, around corners, up wide, sweeping staircases, across echoing, marble-floored halls, prowling through darkened drawing rooms. He passed a few footmen—they reminded him of bees in their black-and-white-striped waistcoats—and even fewer maidservants, clots of royal officials, not to mention bejeweled, perfumed courtiers by the dozens. But no library.

Finally he stopped and looked around. The walls of the hallway he was in were mirrored, showing him reflections upon reflections of his own shabby self. The edges of the mirrors were gilded. A reminder of how wealthy the Kingdom of Aethel had once been—but it was all a bit tarnished now. Dust had collected where the floor met the wall; clearly there weren't quite enough servants to keep it all in order. The kingdom had once been a center of trade, with people from everywhere coming and going at all times, though more recently it had grown isolated from the rest of the world. Not as wealthy, not quite as gilded or great.

The chairs lined up against the walls were gilded, too, and dusty. They were there in case you got tired from wandering lost through the palace, Alex figured. It was, he realized, enormous. What it must cost to heat the place in the winter!

In the nearest mirror he caught a sliver of black, reflected. It wavered, and he turned to see the steward in her black silk dress gliding toward him down the hallway.

"Ah, Librarian Farnsworth," she said briskly.

"Alex," he corrected her.

"Hmm," she murmured. She wore a ring of keys at the end of a chain at her waist, and they jingled as she walked.

"I'm trying to find my way," he said. "This place is huge. It's like a maze."

"Just wait until you see the library," she said with a thin smile. "Come with me."

The steward was short and plump and very correct; she had light brown skin and wore her iron-gray hair in a tight knot at the back of her neck and had deep lines at the corners of her mouth. Lines of disapproval, Alex guessed, not ones she'd gotten from laughing. She disapproved of him, that was for sure.

"When you have guests," he asked, "do you give them a map of this place so they don't get lost?"

"No," she said. "We give them a footman to show them the way."

Well, they weren't going to give *him* a footman. He tried to pay attention as she led him through the palace's winding corridors and echoing chambers until they reached an unobtrusive door set at the end of a deserted hallway with worn carpeting on the floor.

"This is it?" Alex asked.

"It is," the steward replied. She held out a bunch of keys on a heavy iron ring. They ranged from the size of a fingernail to a heavy key as big as his hand.

Librarian keys. Alex felt a prickle of excitement as he took the jangling ring and turned to the door. Sorting through the keys, he found the one that looked like a good match for the lock, and tried it. He turned it, and the door creaked open. Pushing it wider, he peered in. His hands trembled a little with excitement.

A library. *His* library, at least for a while.

It was dim. Tall windows off to the right were covered with velvet curtains, and just a little light filtered in. Spiderwebs were draped around the doorway. He stepped farther in and looked up . . . and up. The room was huge and round, and so far across that every creak of a chair and turn of a page would echo. Bookshelves stretched up the walls, level upon level of them, with balconies and ladders and catwalks, all the way to the ceiling, which was lost in darkness. Alex caught a fluttering movement in the high shadows—were bats living up there?

"Librarian Farnsworth," the steward said from behind him.

He nodded to show that he was listening, while noting that the main floor was made of uncarpeted stone inlaid in some kind of pattern. Two long wooden reading tables with chairs took up half the space. There were also desks and cabinets for the card catalogs, and rows of bookshelves taller than he was made of carved wood, all stuffed with books.

"A warning," the steward said. "This library has been locked since the death of the librarian, nearly a month ago. And before that . . ." Alex glanced back at her and saw that she was frowning. "Maeviss Clark, the librarian, was very, very old, and spent most of her time asleep, or reading. The royal library has been essentially untended for many years." She pointed at the huge room before them. "This is only a small part of it. Sections of it were hacked out of the cliff itself. There are locked rooms that have never, in my time here, been opened. There are rooms that have been found once and never seen again. There are hidden doors. I have heard rumors that one of the librarian's assistants, who disappeared many years ago, is still in here somewhere. In short, there was probably a good reason why the previous librarian made sure she and the pages that served her were holed up in her office most of the time."

The keys weighed heavily in Alex's hand. He felt goose bumps on his arms and tried not to shiver. Looking up, he met the steward's cool gaze. "You're trying to frighten me," he said slowly. Then he added, "It's not going to work."

The steward frowned. "Just as you are a librarian—or

you claim to be—I am a steward. It is my job to know all that goes on in this palace. There *are* dangers here." Her lips thinned into a narrow, disapproving line. "I think it's very likely that you won't live to see the end of your fifteen-day trial. You should get away from here while you still can."

6

Yes, Alex had felt a bolt of blank terror when he'd crested the hill and seen the Winter Palace for the first time. A flash of *What am I getting myself into?*

It had been a four-day journey from Purslane, the pack of supplies that he'd finagled out of the innkeeper was almost empty, and he'd hiked past miles and miles of flat farmland, the rich dirt plowed and ready for winter. In the distance, toward the north, were forested hills, a line of darkness on the horizon. He was passed on the road by courtiers in fine carriages, coming in from their estates to spend the winter at the palace. He walked through quiet country towns where the harvest festival was over. But he hadn't passed many ordinary people. Except for the nobility, the people of Aethel did not travel. They were not curious. They tended to look inward, not outward.

And at the end of his journey, Alex had looked up, and there it was. The Winter Palace.

With the dazzle of the setting sun in his eyes, he thought at first that the palace was a mountain. Or . . . not a mountain exactly. A cliff? It was a huge wedge of rock with a flat top, shaped a bit like a loaf of bread. And, squinting against the sunlight, he'd seen that the royal palace was sort of draped over the entire thing. There was a huge central area at least six stories high, built right into the cliff; it had turrets and galleries of windows with pointed arches over each one, rows of pillars, and a main doorway framed with lavishly carved stone. Banners in black and gold fluttered from every spire. Wide staircases were everywhere, leading down to the gardens, and to rolling hills, which were covered by a city whose buildings seemed tiny, and cowered below the massive palace.

He wasn't stupid; he knew what palaces were for. They weren't like castles or fortresses; they didn't tell the world, *If you bring war to us, we will step on you like a bug.* No, a palace said, *We are powerful beyond measure and we barely even notice your buglike existence.*

Then the setting sun had dipped behind the cliff,

and the palace's shadow fell and darkened the land all around it. And yes, Alex had felt a little like a bug.

But only for a moment. Now that he'd gotten in, past the queen and her steward, he stood in the middle of the library's huge center room and thought back to his view of the palace. One end of it, he remembered, looked older and rougher than the rest. An almost castlelike turret that seemed as if it hadn't been built into the cliff, but that it had grown out of it, like a fat mushroom. The library. He wondered how far into the rock it went. Pretty far, he guessed.

Before she'd left, the steward had made one more thing clear. The queen was the queen, but she, the steward, ran the palace. The queen did not need to know about the state the library was in, and she was not to be bothered. If he had problems, he was to come to her.

Then she had offered him one more chance to leave. A bribe, really. Twenty gold coins to be gone by morning. No one would blame him, she said. It was a bigger job than he could handle; everyone would understand that.

Hah.

Nice try, he thought. But they weren't getting rid of him so easily.

What she didn't seem to understand was that even

though he wasn't Merwyn Farnsworth, he *was*, in fact, an actual librarian, *and* he had something to prove. He could no more leave than, well, than a sea captain could abandon his or her sailors on a sinking ship.

He started across the huge main room, weaving between the heavy wooden tables, his footsteps on the stone floor echoing, and the keys on their ring jangling, until he reached the source of the light that leaked in from outside. Setting down the keys on the nearest table, he grasped the edge of one black velvet curtain with both hands and dragged it back, revealing one narrow window two stories tall. To his dismay, the windowpanes were small, and they were encrusted with probably years of dirt and smudges. When he'd finished pulling back the curtains of the other windows, he surveyed the room again. Still too dim. He'd need a better light source. Especially at night. After sunset, this place would be like a cave.

Time to have a look at the books.

There were, he counted, five levels, with balconies at each one. Spiral staircases led from one level to the next. The railings that edged the balconies and stairs were made of wood, elaborately carved, but scratched and dull with neglect. The air smelled of mold and damp stone.

And the books. Row upon row of them, all shrouded

with dust and jumbled on the shelves, jammed in any which way, all out of order. Gardening manuals next to mathematical treatises next to military histories next to books with pictures in them of fluffy animals, meant for small children. He knew people who would look at these shelves of books and call it *thick wallpaper*, as if they were only for decoration. He knew even more people who would look at the books with narrow-eyed suspicion, but Alex knew what treasure these books really were. His fingers itched to set them straight, to get them cleaned and cataloged and organized. He could imagine what the room would look like with plenty of light, the wood polished, the books dusted, their leather covers oiled and gleaming. It would glow golden. It would be the greatest library in the world.

Not that anyone would see it, or read its books.

He surveyed the main room again, and spotted an arched doorway that, he found, led into a smaller circular room with a much lower ceiling. Opening the curtains in that room, he saw a desk piled with books, papers, empty teacups, all of it coated with dust. He set down the keys among the clutter and surveyed the rest of the room. The walls were lined with shelves that were crammed with books. There was a couch that had once been luxuriously covered with red velvet, but was now faded and patched, with tufts of stuffing leaking out. A ratty, lumpy pillow sat at one end. The floor was covered with a flowered rug, also filthy and dusty.

Circling the desk, he pulled out the carved wooden chair and sat in it.

The librarian's office. *His* office.

What would Pa say if he could see him now?

Alex couldn't help remembering their last argument.

Pa had shouted. The dark brown skin of his face had been flushed with anger—only Alex had the ability to set him off that badly. And then Alex had shouted something even worse, something maybe unforgivable, and he had stalked out of his pa's office. He had kept going, out of his home and down the road, and he wasn't going back. Ever.

Right.

He should probably do something . . . librarianish.

He rooted around in the papers and books on the desk until he found what he was looking for. A light-well, which was a chunk of translucent rock about the size of his fist. If it was left out in the sun during the day, it soaked in the sunlight and then gave it back again, slowly, as a warm, golden glow. Any proper librarian knew that light-wells were the only things used for light in a library.

This light-well was empty and dark. Taking it with

him, he got to his feet and left the office, going to stand in the exact center of the main room.

For a long moment, all was quiet. He could practically hear the dust settling. The things that had been flying around earlier in the shadows of the high ceiling had gone still. The silence grew heavier. The bracelet of words around his wrist tightened with anticipation. His ears prickled with listening.

And then, *then* he heard it.

The sound started near the ceiling, at the very highest shelves, the fifth level of balconies. A rustling, as of pages turning. The noise grew louder, the sound like the rush of a waterfall flowing down from one level to the next, rustling, bumping, an even louder thumping.

Alex's mouth felt dry. Dust sifted down around him, glinting in the dim light like silver snow. Echoes filled the room, making his ears ring. He checked the letters printed on his wrist to see if they spelled out anything he could use to settle the books, but they were a jumble, forming no words. Clenching his fists, he willed his voice not to crack when he spoke. "All right," he said steadily. "That's enough."

Abruptly, the noise stopped.

He took a deep breath. This library had been locked up, undisturbed, since the librarian had died. It should be quiet and still and safe.

But it was not.

Alex had been marked by the Red Codex, and he'd been attacked at Purslane Castle, so he'd had good reasons to suspect that something strange was happening to books. They were alive, he realized with a sudden, bone-deep certainty. Books were *alive*. Not just the dangerous ones; *all* books were alive. Sort of. Not like people, but in some strange, bookish way. They had been asleep, and now they were waking up.

Why were they waking up?

He didn't know.

Had they woken up before, sometime in the distant past? They *must* have. That would explain why libraries felt creepy to most people. The old librarians had to know that books were alive—this was one of their secrets. Maybe these guardians kept their libraries locked to keep people out *and* to keep the books in.

Maybe . . . oh, here was a snaky idea. Maybe books woke up when they were read.

A book is more dangerous than any sword, he'd told the queen. He knew he'd been exaggerating. But what if it was true?

Was this library truly dangerous? Was it a danger to him? And to anyone who came into it?

He wasn't sure. But he knew one thing. It was time to get to work.

The question that bothered him was, *what* work? Alex wasn't sure how librarians dealt with books that were, quite probably, alive in some way. Putting them in order might help settle them. Cataloging. So that's where he started.

He spent a few days poking around the main room of the library, looking through the catalog—a card for every book, filed in small, square drawers with brass knobs. The cards were an annoyingly jumbled mess. Putting them back in order would take months.

Time he didn't have, for a lot of reasons.

One afternoon he left the big main room of the library and made his way through winding passages and arched doorways, past too many rooms to count that were stuffed with books and maps and unbound manuscripts, and scrolls, and heavy tomes a foot thick, and tiny books that would fit into the palm of his hand. As he passed the shelves, with the golden glow of a light-well spilling out before him, the books rustled and bumped. Some of them were secured to the shelves, and they rattled their chains as he passed, and others thumped against the bars that caged them.

It was almost as if they were jostling for his attention.

"I'll get to you," he promised them as he walked past. But he had to survey the rest of the library first. See what else he had to deal with here.

The steward hadn't been wrong. The library *was* a maze, one he could easily get lost in. And it was dark—he needed light to see what he was doing. He paused to take a book off a shelf in a passage not far from the main room, just to check if it had been read any time recently. It was positively coated with dust, and the spine cracked as he opened it. It almost nestled into his hands—a book by an author named G. V. Eek about a pack of dogs flying a ship into space, of all things—as if it was grateful to be read.

Alex had set the light-well on a nearby shelf. As he read, the light flickered. Its golden glow dimmed.

Alex picked it up and examined it. As an apprentice at Purslane Castle, one of his duties had been to collect all the light-wells in the library every week or two and take them outside to be refilled with sunlight.

The only other jobs the librarian would let him do were sweeping the floor, cleaning the windows, and dusting the shelves. Farnsworth wouldn't trust Alex with any actual books—at least, not at first.

And now that he knew books were *alive*, he could see why.

Alex figured Farnsworth hadn't entirely trusted

him because of the words printed on his wrist. When he'd arrived at the castle, he'd made the mistake of showing the jumbled letters to the librarian, who had stared at them, shocked. "You've been marked?" Farnsworth had asked. "How?"

Alex told him about the Red Codex in his father's library, though he was careful not to mention his father's name. He described how the letters had flowed out of the book onto his skin and rearranged themselves to form words.

Farnsworth had taken Alex's left hand in his bony, papery hand and turned it over, peering at his wrist. "What words?"

"*Book*," Alex had told him. "Then *stolen, the, never,* and *codex.*"

"*Codex?*" Farnsworth had looked up quickly, blinking rapidly. "*The* codex?" He shook his head. "No. Surely not. Surely not."

Alex had pulled his hand away from the old man and tugged his sleeve to cover his wrist. "What is a codex, exactly?" He'd wondered about that for a long time.

"It's a book, that's all," Farnsworth had said. "*Codex* is another word for a book. Any book." Then the old man had muttered something under his breath that sounded like "*But it was not the codex, surely.*" Then he added, "Erm, well." His voice wavered. "I, ah, suppose you'd better stay here where I can keep an eye on you."

Alex had known better than to ask him what he'd meant by *the* Codex. He'd been marked by it, that's all he knew. After that, he tried to keep the bracelet of words more of a secret.

Alex had stayed at the Purslane library, and had done boring cleaning chores at first. Gradually the librarian had entrusted him with other book-related jobs, and taught him way too much about bug poop . . . but he'd never told Alex any librarian secrets.

Anyway, thanks to his time at Purslane, Alex knew an empty light-well when he saw one, and this one was about to go dark. The light flickered again, and he reshelved the book about space dogs, giving it a comforting pat before he left it, making his way through the winding passages and past the rustling books, back to where he'd started. Night had fallen outside, and the big main room was dark, and seemed even more echoingly huge than it had when he'd first arrived. He felt tiny, with his little spark of light, trudging through the tall shadows.

And then he heard footsteps. The sound of them echoed in the big room, so he couldn't tell where they were coming from. The fourth level, maybe.

"Hello?" he called, and raised the fading light-well.

The footsteps stopped.

Alex peered up into the darkness. Was someone up there, looking back at him? "Who's there?" he said sharply, crossing to the stairway. As he paused on the bottom step, he heard the sound of footsteps, running, and then a door slammed. He tensed, ready to race up the stairs and chase the intruder. *Nobody* should be in here.

The library settled into silence again.

Tonight it was too late and too dark. Tomorrow he'd go up and look for footprints in the dust. Wearily, Alex set down the light-well on the nearest table and stretched his arms over his head.

He hadn't held a sword since he left home. But a long time ago he'd promised his pa that he would never miss a day of training. Even at Purslane Castle, even on the road to the Winter Palace, he never had. It wasn't just because his pa was completely honorable and had taught him to keep his promises; he also trained every day because if the books really were alive and waking up, he'd need to be ready for anything—even for something dangerous to happen. So, in the middle of the stone floor of the library, he sparred with an imaginary weapon against an imaginary opponent, then ran through a few agility drills, just to keep himself sharp. That done, he wiped the sweat off his face with his sleeve and crossed the room to the library door where, on the steward's orders, a servant left his meals on a tray out in the hallway.

Unlocking the door, Alex collected the tray and—after locking the door again—he carried it into the librarian's office. Setting down the flickering light-well, he examined the food.

His pa would have something to say about plain bread and cheese. Given such a thing, Pa would roar and bluster, and a far better dinner would be brought to him. Then he would share most of it with the Family, and even if there wasn't much it would seem like a feast because Pa was there, and dinner would be followed by stories and singing, probably, and spitting contests, and Jeffen would challenge Franciss to an arm-wrestle, and they'd all bet on the outcome, but not with money, with dessert, assuming there was any.

Alex was too tired to complain about bread and cheese, or to think any more about people who he would miss with a constant ache, if he was the kind of person who missed other people. Which he was not. No, he wasn't even the remotest, tiniest bit homesick. He didn't miss Jeffen's teasing, or Franciss's nonsensical sayings, or the rest of the noisy, rowdy, not-at-all-bookish Family. He didn't miss the way, no matter how busy his pa was, he found time every night to sit on the edge of the bed and listen while Alex told him about his day. From the time he was a tiny kid, Alex had often been too overwrought to sleep, too full of fire and frustration, and only Pa could settle him and make everything all right. Then Pa would kiss him on the forehead and say, "I'll see you in the morning, son."

The light-well flickered out. In the dark, Alex ate the food, and a lonely apple he'd saved from breakfast, and then felt his way to the lumpy couch where he'd slept for the last few nights. With a prickle of unease, he realized that the previous librarian had probably died there. Maybe she'd died of old age, as the steward had said. Alex figured it was a lot more likely that the librarian had been reading a book that had attacked her, and killed her.

A book that was still in the royal library. Somewhere.

7

"My dear, this simply will not do," her uncle said.

Kenneret stood before the desk in his office. Her steward, Dorriss, waited quietly by the door.

The room was done up all in warm golds and yellows with black trim, the colors of the Kingdom of Aethel. Her uncle sat behind his desk with his elbows on the black, lacquered wood, his chin resting on folded hands. Behind him was a shelf that had his collection of figurines arranged carefully on it, with not a speck of dust on them. She eyed them as he studied her. There was a snarling bronze cat, a graceful woman dancing in alabaster, an intricately carved ivory ball, and a funny little bearded man holding a frog made of gold. That one was new, she thought.

"Are you paying attention?" her uncle prompted.

She blinked. "Yes, of course, Uncle Patch," she replied. He was a little like a figurine himself, she realized. He was polished and perfect in his yellow silk coat, always with a faint smile on his face. Not a hair out of place because he didn't have any hair, not even any eyebrows or eyelashes.

"As I was saying," he said patiently, "it will not do to have half the courtiers in the palace freezing to death this winter."

Drat. She knew her uncle wouldn't be happy about this. "The cost of heating the palace is very high," she started to explain. "I don't think—"

"A necessary expense," her uncle interrupted.

She *hated* it when he interrupted her. "Twenty thousand golds," she began again. "It's a ridiculous amount of money. And even with the courtiers here, half the rooms in the palace are empty. Why heat them? It doesn't make any sense!" By the time she finished speaking, she was so frustrated that her voice was shaking.

Instead of answering her question, her uncle shook his head. "Now, what have I taught you, Kennie, about losing control?"

"This is important to me," she insisted.

"And that is not a bad thing." Uncle Patch stood and circled the desk, coming to stand beside her, where he took her hand in his. "My dear, you have been queen for only a few months. You are surrounded by people who dislike you simply because you have power and they do not. You *must* be in control at all times. In control of yourself, and in control of your emotions. You cannot smile because you are happy—you smile to indicate royal approval of carefully selected courtiers. You should never frown unless it is politically expedient to do so. Your voice must never shake as it did just now."

Kenneret felt a flush of embarrassment mixed with anger creeping up her face. And of course he noticed.

With a gentle finger, he tapped her cheek. "Your emotions—anger, happiness, frustration, loneliness, even love—must never betray you. They are a tool to be used wisely."

She took a steadying breath. Was this how it was for him? He was always so mild, and kind, trying to help her.

She had only been queen for a short time. After her mother, the queen of Aethel, had died, ten years ago, Uncle Patch had raised her and her brother, Charlie, while serving as regent—ruling the kingdom until

Kenneret was old enough to take over. He had taught her everything she knew about being queen. Though lately . . .

. . . his critiques had become a lot more pointed . . .

. . . and Kenneret was beginning to have her own ideas about what it meant to be queen. Ideas she wasn't quite ready to talk to him about. She knew he wouldn't approve.

"Now, about the heating costs," Uncle Patch said, dropping her hand and going back to sit behind his desk. "I think the royal exchequer can come up with twenty thousand golds to keep us all from freezing in our beds this winter. Don't you?"

Kenneret didn't answer. What answer could she give that would not reveal her emotions?

From over by the door came the faintest rustle, a reminder that her steward was waiting, and watching.

"Kennie," Uncle Patch said, and the faintest trace of carefully calculated impatience crept into his voice. "Aethel was once a great kingdom, one of the wealthiest in the world. We have become a nation of farmers with our noses in the dirt. You need to have your mind on bigger issues, my dear, than the cost of a few warm fires in the palace hearths. You need to have vision. The fate of the kingdom is at stake."

The lesson about being a good queen was one that

she had heard many times before. But this *fate of the kingdom* thing was new. She wondered what *bigger issues* he meant. Instead of commenting on that, she gave him a faint smile. Emotions in check.

"Very good," her uncle said, and gave her a nod of approval and of dismissal. "Thank you, my dear."

Kenneret left the office, her steward closing the door softly behind them.

Her uncle had summoned her just as she'd been about to leave for one of her regular meetings with the sword master at the practice hall. As they hurried through the mirrored hallways of the palace, past bowing servants and curtseying courtiers, Kenneret glanced aside at the steward, who had her usual disapproving look on her face.

"Well?" Kenneret asked as they crossed a reception hall that had a marble floor badly in need of a polish. "What's the matter?"

"Her Majesty is queen," Dorriss said through tight lips. "Lord Patchedren should not summon the queen to his office. If he wishes to speak to the queen, he should attend her in *her* office."

Kenneret blinked. "Well, he is my uncle, after all, Dorriss."

"*And* he should address the queen as *Your Majesty*, not as *my dear* or by a pet name he gave her as a child."

Kenneret felt like laughing. But she didn't, of course. Because her steward was giving her basically the same advice that her uncle had.

She knew exactly what they meant—don't be a niece who obeys the uncle who raised her. Don't be a girl who worries that twenty thousand golds could feed a lot of people during a cold winter. Don't be a girl who laughs at the ridiculousness of the royal *we*.

Be queen.

8

Alex had to admit that the job was too much for him.

He needed help. An assistant. Or a page, at least, one of the magical pieces of paper that obeyed a librarian's every order and helped keep the books in line. Even better would be a whole team of librarians, but he knew that was pointless. On his travels Alex had discovered two things. One, librarians were loners. In every single library he'd visited after he'd left home there was just one librarian, along with a page or two and a few assistants.

The second thing he'd learned was that librarians were old. Every librarian that Alex had met was like

Merwyn Farnsworth. Ancient. And they weren't interested in training up apprentices, either. They knew
secret bookish things, but they weren't telling.

Librarians, then, were dying out.

Alex wondered if all libraries were becoming like
this one—full of books that had gone feral and moldy
and restless. No sooner did Alex get one section organized and cataloged than another fell into disarray.
And there were any number of rooms that he hadn't
even gone into yet. Everything was out of alphabetical
order. It *bothered* him.

Clearly it bothered the books, too. Or *something*
did.

All the books from the avian room of the royal
library were flapping lazily around the high ceiling
of the main room. On the first day he'd tried luring
them with bread crumbs, and then he'd captured
them, but as soon as he left their room they were off
the shelves and flying around again. They were joined
at night by the books about bats. If that wasn't snaky
enough, the romance novels kept hurling themselves
off their shelves like unrequited lovers jumping from
cliffs. Even weirder, the architecture books had shut
themselves into a series of rooms. From inside came
sounds of shelves being shifted, and once Alex heard

the grumble of stones being dragged across the floor. Who knew what they were up to? Barricading themselves in—but against what?

Quite often Alex had the creepy, prickly feeling that he was being watched. He hadn't found any trace of whoever had been walking around in the dark the other night, and the main door to the library was always locked. Maybe he had imagined it?

No, don't be stupid, Alex told himself. Somebody was lurking around.

But he couldn't worry about it now—there were more pressing things. The door of one room off the fourth-floor balcony had been blocked off with sandbags, piled high from floor to ceiling. There was probably something dangerous inside, Alex figured, but it was better to find out sooner rather than later what it was, exactly. The sandbags were heavy, almost more than he could lift. One by one, he shifted them aside, lugging them out to the balcony and stacking them there.

Strength training, his pa would call it. A blasted nuisance, more like.

Once the door was clear, Alex opened it and peered inside, raising the light-well to see better. It wasn't even a room, he thought, more a closet. Sandbags lined the walls inside. In the middle of the closet, wrapped in chains that were secured to a stone block, was a square, fat book with its title embossed in bold, block letters.

ON THE CHEMISTRY OF BLACKPOWDER EXPLOSIONS

The book had a sturdy metal latch riveted to its cover, and a small padlock held it closed. As Alex bent to examine the keyhole, the book suddenly lunged toward him and Alex leaped back quickly.

"Gah!" he gasped, just as the chains brought the book up short.

Rattle, rattle, rattle—the book seethed like a pot of boiling water with a fire under it. Take the lid off the pot, and *boom*.

Alex figured he must have a key for the padlock. Not that he was going to actually open the book—he wasn't an idiot—but he wanted to be sure. He'd left the heavy ring of keys on the desk in his office. Closing the door to the blackpowder book's closet, he went down the spiral staircase, fetched the keys, and was headed back across the wide stone floor when he thought he heard a noise.

He froze in the middle of the huge circular room and cocked his head, listening.

The books on the second level were shifting on their shelves. Not a big fuss, just a subtle rustling of pages.

Curious, Alex climbed up to the second-floor balcony, then halfway around to the fourth passage leading off of it. There were no windows—this part of the library was dug out of the cliff—but he could see light coming from farther along the passageway.

On silent feet, Alex headed toward the light. It wasn't from a candle—not open flame, but something stronger. Rounding a corner, he came upon a man taking a book from a shelf.

"What are you doing in my library?" Alex asked abruptly.

The man, whoever he was, set the book back on the shelf and turned to smile at Alex without showing his teeth. He was completely bald, his head shiny, like polished wood. He didn't have any eyebrows, either, or eyelashes. He wore gloves covering his hands. His frock coat was made of yellow silk, embroidered with glistening seed pearls. All very fine and fancy. And out of place among the dusty, cobweb-covered books.

Some random courtier, Alex assumed.

"This is *your* library?" the man asked in an unexpectedly deep, resonant voice. He held up a fully charged light-well and looked Alex over, from head to toe.

"Yes," Alex said. "I'm a librarian. The door to the library is locked. How did you get in here?"

The man would have raised his brows if he had them; instead he just lifted the skin over his eyes. "Surely you are mistaken," he said smoothly. "The door was open."

"No," Alex snapped. "I'm not mistaken." He was *very* careful about the locks in the library. He didn't want random people wandering around, making the books more unsettled than they already were. "Wait." He narrowed his eyes. "You were here the other night, weren't you? Sneaking around in the dark."

"Sneaking?" the man exclaimed. "Surely I don't look like someone who sneaks!" Before Alex could spit out an answer to that, the man waved a hand as if shooing away a pesky fly, and said, "Never mind. We won't dwell on your irresponsibility in leaving the door unlocked. I was told that the name of the new royal librarian was Merwyn Farnsworth. You, I assume?"

"That's right," Alex lied.

"*Really*," the man said, drawing out the word. "I thought I met a librarian named Farnsworth many years ago. An old man, even then. But perhaps I am the one mistaken this time?"

"And you were mistaken before, too," Alex insisted. "The library door was locked." He held up the ring of keys he was carrying and jingled it, to prove his point.

The man gave his toothless smile again. "My good-ness, you *are* persistent. And a bit young for this job, don't you think?"

Alex felt his temper flare up. He opened his mouth to say something that would probably get him into trouble. Then he stopped. The passageway they were in was lined with shelves. All of the books, he realized, had gone absolutely still. Almost as if they were afraid. Their silence and stillness had that sort of cowering feel to it.

Something else was going on here. Taking a deep breath, Alex shoved his temper aside. "I'll take you to the door," he said evenly, "so you can leave."

The man looked faintly amused, as if Alex had said something funny, which he definitely had not. He inclined his head gracefully and let Alex lead him down the passage and out to the balcony that over-looked the main room of the library.

Instead of preceding Alex down one of the spiral staircases, the man went to the railing that edged the balcony. It was intricately carved, but covered with dust. Fastidiously, the man brushed at the railing with his gloved fingers, then leaned over to survey the library. "So many books," he said, almost idly. "It is rather a large job, isn't it?"

"I can manage it," Alex replied, knowing full well that he couldn't. Trying to make it seem as if it didn't matter, he leaned an elbow on the balcony rail.

The man looked around. "I don't see any pages. Surely you have one or two, like every proper librarian?"

"Not at the moment," Alex said. His lack of pages was a problem, he knew it, and he didn't need this flippant man to remind him about it.

"Ah. You are so young and, one can assume, inexperienced." The man's voice dripped with concern. "It is clear that the royal library is too much for you."

"I told you I can manage it," Alex said, getting irritated again.

"Of *course* you can." The man was all condescension. "Well, I shall take my leave of you now, Librarian *Farnsworth*. I am certain that we shall meet again soon."

Leaning on the balcony, Alex watched him go down the winding stairway. The man was carrying the fully charged light-well, so he was surrounded by a yellow glow as he crossed the main floor.

Wait for him to reach the door, Alex told himself.

The door *had* been locked. Alex was absolutely certain. He was ready to go down with his jingling ring of keys to let the man out. He even had a barbed comment ready to go for when he would slam the door in the man's face.

But, after pausing to send another patronizing glance in Alex's direction, the man opened the door and left.

Scowling, Alex went down the spiral staircase and stalked across the stone floor. At the door, he sorted through the keys until he found the right one.

Too young, the man had said. *No pages. Irresponsible. Inexperienced.* And *I once met an old man named Farnsworth, and you are clearly not him.*

Strictly speaking, all of those things were true. Alex had a feeling they were supposed to make him feel inadequate, and maybe even stupid. Instead, they made him pay attention. They put a little edge on him.

Alex had absolutely no doubt. He had *not* left the library door unlocked. Something else was at work here.

He didn't know who this man was, but clearly he was up to something.

As his frustration grew, Alex realized that he was rubbing his left wrist. Pushing up the sleeve of his shirt, he checked the bracelet of letters.

They were moving, shifting, climbing over each other like ants. As he watched, holding his breath, the letters rearranged themselves until they spelled out a word. And the word was . . .

KEYS.

9

Keys.

He wasn't sure what it meant, beyond the obvious. Yes, he had a key to the library, and somehow that sly courtier did, too. But what else could it be? Some kind of warning?

With his finger he rubbed at the black letters that spelled out **KEYS** against his pale skin. The letters didn't smudge, like ink. It was as if they were printed on a page. And then, the letters started tingling again, shifted, and stilled. Now they spelled nothing at all.

Alex watched them for another minute to see if they'd tell him anything else. Which they didn't. "Blast it," he muttered, and took his own set of keys and locked the door behind the courtier, whoever he was. Then he went straight back to the room where he'd left the book about blackpowder explosions. Checking the ring to be sure that he had the key to the padlock holding the book closed—he did—he shut the door to the closet, locked it, and piled the sandbags in front of it again. The library was unsettled, that was for sure. If this particular book was affected, the results could be . . . well . . . explosive.

While he worked, he tried not to dwell on what *keys* meant, or on what the courtier had said. He hated that the man had so easily seen through him. It was *so* glaringly obvious that Alex was in over his head and, maybe, didn't know what a librarian's real job was. But he wasn't going to panic. No. One of the many things he'd learned from his pa was that anything worth doing took time. You couldn't just train with the sword one afternoon a week and hope to get anywhere. No, you trained for hours every day; you took sword fighting apart, down to its most basic elements, and you put it back together, and then, after years of work, maybe you'd be ready to train with edged blades instead of heavy wooden practice swords. And then, if you ever got into a real fight, you wouldn't be killed by your opponent within the first thirty seconds.

One book at a time, he told himself, and got back to work.

Later that day, on the third-tier balcony, he found a room that held mostly cookbooks with, oddly, some books about natural disasters mixed in. *Cakes* and *quakes,* he guessed—somebody had mis-shelved them. Carefully he pulled out all the disaster books and stacked them by the arched doorway to be put in their proper place. Turning, he picked up his fading light-well and started to leave the room, when he heard a *bump-thump* from one of the shelves. He went to inspect the source of the noise.

A History of the Earthquakes of Xan read the spine of the book. "Sorry," he told it. "Almost left you behind." He took the book off the shelf and carried it to the pile of books at the door.

He was just about to set it down when he saw its cover. Smooth brown leather edged with brassy gold, and in the center . . .

He caught his breath. It looked like the same exact symbol he'd seen on the book that Merwyn

Farnsworth was reading when he'd died.

Or, Alex suspected, when he'd been killed.

The same book that had attacked him, too.

He gazed down at the book in his hands. It seemed ordinary. There was no sense of creeping evil. The cover was worn, as if it had been read many times. It looked harmless.

But it was heavy. Too heavy for a book its size.

Alex ran a finger down the edge of the front cover. He *really* wanted to open it. Would it be like the *Vines: Plants of Wonder* book that had, maybe, killed Master Farnsworth? After reading the first page, would the book *actually* try to kill him?

"I'm a librarian," he said to himself. "I can do this."

He'd been trained as a soldier, after all. He knew how to fight. The same rules applied, if you thought about it, to books and to swords. For one thing, you didn't run away from a challenge. You met it, head-on. His pa had taught him that.

If he was ready for it, he could hold the book off. All he had to do was close his eyes, and he would stop reading. He knew he needed to see what was in there. He needed to get the measure of this book, to figure out what it was, exactly, because he was certain that it was much more than just a book about earthquakes in faraway Xan.

Carefully he turned the book to face him. He held it, ready to open.

The room he was in went still. The books on the shelves around him had gone deathly quiet. Even the light-well had dimmed. The letters printed on the skin of his wrist tingled just the slightest bit, almost in warning.

"Don't be an idiot, Alex," he told himself. *"Put the book down."*

And then he opened it.

The first page was blank. As he stared, the charred symbol appeared, expanding to fill the entire page, outlined in ember-colored fire. It smelled of smoke and rotten eggs. The symbol seemed to pulse, drawing his eyes. Almost against his will, Alex reached up, took the corner of the next page, and turned it.

And in that second the book came after him.

The words came in a rush—no faint numbness in his fingertips this time, no—before he could even blink, they had him. Words snatched at him, swirling around him. They whispered and howled. The ground under his feet started to shake—an earthquake, happening right there in the room with him! His hands went numb, and then as cold as ice. All around him, the books were being shaken off the shelves. The stones in the walls started to shift.

And he couldn't move.

Then, with a groan, one of the shelves ripped away from the wall, sending books flying in every direction. They pummeled at Alex like heavy fists, and then the shelf crashed to the floor right before him. An inch closer, and he would have been crushed.

The quake grew worse, and the stones under his feet started bucking and creaking.

Without his pa's training, he would have panicked, but he knew how to keep control of himself in a fight. With the last fading scrap of himself, he managed to slam the book closed. It dropped from his fingers and landed on the ground.

Shaking too much to stand, Alex followed it down. He sat with his head on his bent knees. The room fell suddenly still. As the floor stopped moving, a last bit of dust sifted down from the ceiling.

The book lay before him.

The symbol was scorched even more deeply into its cover.

Slowly, without taking his eyes from the book, Alex climbed to his feet. He picked up the light-well, backed out of the room, closed the door, and with trembling hands, locked it. He leaned against a wall, feeling sick and shaky.

The last royal librarian had died mysteriously, and

Alex was willing to bet it was because she had picked up a book just like that one. It had attacked her, and she hadn't been ready for it, and so it had killed her.

There were, he felt certain, more books hidden in the library with that strange symbol on their cover. No books of any kind were ordinary. He'd figured that much out. But the marked books—somehow, they had been changed.

Every single one of them had become a trap.

Wondering about the symbol and what it meant, Alex made his way to the main room. Leaning on the balcony at the third level, he surveyed the library by the faint glow of the light-well. It was cavernous. The dusty air trembled; there was a low rustling noise. The books were restless. They knew what had just happened.

They were afraid.

Of what?

Maybe they didn't want to be marked with the symbol. "I'll try to protect you," he told them.

Wait. What had he just said? *Protect.* "Ohhhh," he breathed. *That* was what a librarian was, he realized, and he wanted to curse himself for being so slow to figure it out. A librarian was not just a cataloger, a sweeper, a duster, a collector of frass, an alphabetizer, a keeper of keys. A librarian was a *protector.* Of books.

A heavy, watching silence fell. He waited.

From the corner of his eye, he caught a flash of movement. He couldn't help it, he flinched, and the thing he'd seen disappeared again. Carefully, he straightened and held himself absolutely still.

And then he caught a glimpse of something floating just behind his left shoulder. A square of white. A single page. Shyly, it edged closer. He stayed quiet and still, and the page floated through the air, undulating as if it was swimming through water like a fish, coming to hang in the air at his eye level. Three more pages joined it.

"Hello," he whispered.

As he watched, a word took shape on the first page, as if it was being written by an invisible hand with an invisible pen, thin, wavery, inky lines against the stark white of the paper.

Librarian, he read.

"Yes," he whispered. He waited, holding his breath, and more words appeared.

Librarian, we are your pages. We await your orders.

He let himself feel a moment of fierce pride— Yes! His own pages! By fighting off the earthquake book, he'd proven himself to them—he *was* a librarian!

It was the pages' job to help him. He knew they were simple creatures. He couldn't say to them, *Go find out what's marking the books in the library with that snaky symbol.* They could only carry messages and take specific, concrete orders. And he knew just where they could start. He held up the light-well, which was down to its last flicker. "Pages, are there any more of these around?"

We will search the library, wrote the page. With a rustle, it flitted away, joined by two others. They swooped through the cavernous room like white birds, flew into a passage, and were gone.

10

The next morning, there was a pile of empty light-wells waiting for him on the desk. One by one, Alex examined them.

"Blast it," he said aloud when he'd finished. Every single light-well was dead. They'd been left in the dark corners of the library for too long, and none of them would take in any more sunlight.

Well, this would never do. He needed to talk to the queen.

The pages had brought him some other things. On a table next to the window he found a bowl of water, still warm, a bar of soap, and a fluffy towel with a crown embroidered on it in gold thread.

"Is that a hint?" he asked the pages that were hovering nearby. Sniffing his armpit, he decided that it probably was. He needed a wash.

But first things first.

The books in the royal library were waking up. Some of them had been marked and were decidedly dangerous. He didn't know why and he didn't know how, but he was the one who would be dealing with them, while protecting the other books as best he could. At least, for the next ten days he would, according to the queen.

So he ran through his weaponless sword training, and did his footwork and agility drills, spending extra time on it, until he was panting and dripping with sweat. He could imagine his pa scoffing at how soft he'd gotten. He needed to stay sharp.

Then he washed up and found that the pages had delivered clothes, which they'd left draped over the chair at his desk. Everything was too big, but the trousers came with a belt, and it was all clean. To top it all off, they'd brought a frock coat made of brown velvet, with tarnished gold braid at the cuffs and at the edge of the high collar. It was a bit worn, secondhand. He put it on and turned up the sleeves so it fit better. The coat had the royal bear and shovel and sword embroidered in gold thread on the front of it, topped by a golden crown.

A page edged up to him, almost shyly, and dropped something at his feet.

A woolly hat with a red pompon on top.

Alex bent and picked it up. "Thanks," he said, wondering where the pages had gotten it, along with the rest of the clothes.

Pulling the hat over his untidy hair, he headed toward the library door. It took all of his willpower not to stop and read every single book on the shelves that he passed. He *loved* reading—loved taking a neglected book off the shelf and opening it, smelling its book smell, feeling the smooth pages under his fingers. When he read, it felt like the words were like rain falling on thirsty earth. They did something in his head—they made things grow in there. He'd been too busy for reading. That would have to change. Once he got all of this trouble with the marked books settled . . .

If it didn't settle him, that is.

With a regretful shake of his head, he left the library, carefully locking the door behind him and putting the key into his coat pocket. He started down the long hallway and came out into a corridor busy with people dressed in clothes far finer than his own, and also footmen and maidservants in their black-and-gold uniforms, along with other servants carrying buckets of coal or firewood or cleaning supplies.

He snagged the first footman who passed him. "Take me to the queen," he ordered.

The redheaded footman, who wore a black-and-gold-striped waistcoat that made him look like a honeybee, gave Alex an astonished look. "Huh?"

"The queen," Alex said impatiently. "You know, the one who's in charge of all of this." He waved his hand, taking in the hallway and all the people, but meaning the palace—and beyond.

"Ri-ight," said the footman slowly. "The one who's in charge." He looked Alex up and down. "You're the new librarian?" At Alex's nod, he shrugged. "This way, then."

Alex followed as the footman led him through mirrored passages that he remembered from when he'd first arrived, past the office where he'd met the queen, down another staircase, to a room with a heavy wooden door standing open. The footman paused there, knocked on the open door, and leaned in. "Someone to see you, ma'am," he said. "All right if I show him in?" He must have gotten a nod in return, because he stood aside, gave Alex a nasty smile, and said, "Go ahead."

Taking a deep breath, Alex stepped into the office

and saw—not the queen. It was the steward, sitting at a desk piled with papers. Two secretary-like men stood behind her, as if awaiting her orders.

"Ah, Librarian," the steward said, setting down her pen. "It has only been five days. Giving up already?"

"What?" Alex asked. He shook his head. "No."

"Well, then. What do you want?"

She had already tried getting rid of him once. He wasn't going to talk to her. "I wanted to see the queen." He glanced at the door, but the footman had gone. "But I was brought here instead."

"Her Royal Majesty is busy this morning," the steward said smoothly.

"Oh." Alex remembered something else. "And I wanted to talk to you, too." He fixed her with his most deadly gaze.

Calmly, she folded her hands on her desk. "Yes?"

She was still breathing, so clearly the gaze wasn't deadly enough. "Somebody else has keys to the library," he said.

"No, there is only one set of keys," she replied.

"Someone," Alex insisted, "a man—a courtier, I think—has been sneaking around in my library. So there must be another set of keys."

"There is not," she said, and she sounded absolutely sure about it. "The only keys are on the ring that you were given. Well, and a key for the main library door, which is in my possession at all times." She stood and jingled the set of keys she wore on a chain at her waist. "Now, will that be all?"

"No," Alex answered. "I told you. I need to talk to the queen."

"And I believe I told *you*," the steward answered, sitting down again, "that she is busy this morning."

Alex kept a grip on his temper. "I'm the royal librarian. She'll see me."

The steward raised a faintly amused eyebrow. "The servants have been given orders. You are not to see the queen. They will not take you to her."

"Fine," Alex said through gritted teeth. "Page!" he ordered.

There was a long, awkward moment where nothing happened.

Then, slowly, one of his pages materialized at his shoulder. It was barely visible, just the faintest outline of a page, but it was definitely there.

"Take me to Queen Kenneret," Alex ordered.

And as the steward stared, her mouth dropping open with astonishment, Alex spun on his heel and left her office, following his page. He tried to slam the door behind him, but it was too heavy.

11

Alex's page floated before him, leading him through the palace until they reached a side door that opened to the outside. There, a wide stone stairway led down to a huge, walled garden that was spread out below the castle. Beyond it, the city began.

Alex stood on the steps and surveyed the garden. Near its center was a two-story greenhouse with fogged-up windows. Nearer he could see vegetable beds that were only humps of dirt now that winter had arrived, gravel paths, and little ponds slicked with ice, statues with moss growing on them, and bushes trimmed into elaborate shapes, like bears and other wild animals, with here and there a pumpkin or an ear of corn to keep things interesting. Just coming around the corner of a high hedge was a group of people, all dressed in finery that, he knew, was supposed to reflect the wealth and prosperity of a kingdom that hadn't been all that wealthy or prosperous for the last sixty years.

Taking a deep breath, Alex rushed down the last few steps and onto a gravel path. He had time to glimpse the queen in the center of the group, her head cocked as if she was listening to something the woman next to her was saying, when he was suddenly seized from behind.

"Back off," he snarled at the guard who had grabbed him.

The guard responded by trying to twist Alex's arm up behind his back.

A moment later, the guard was on the ground, moaning and clutching his tender bits.

His father had at least twenty men-at-arms living with him at all times. Alex knew how to get out of a grip when he wanted to.

With gravel crunching under his feet, Alex went along the path to meet the group of people. He heard rapid footsteps coming from behind him and got ready to fight off another guard when the queen lifted a bejeweled hand. "Let him pass," she said to the guard.

He gave Alex a dirty look. Alex returned it, with

interest. They'd settle up later, he guessed. The guard bowed to the queen and went to help the other guard get on his feet, then they went and took up menacingly alert positions nearby.

Queen Kenneret was examining Alex, her face carefully blank. He hadn't seen her standing up before, only sitting. She was, he realized, shorter than he was by quite a bit. It made him feel gleeful, and he wanted to make a rude remark about it, but he didn't. *You won't get what you want by being obnoxious,* he reminded himself.

So instead, he bowed.

"Royal Librarian," she greeted him.

He straightened. This was going well so far. "I need to talk to you, Your Majesty."

She gave him a tight smile. "Go ahead, Librarian Farnsworth. Or perhaps we should call you Temporary Librarian? Or Interim Librarian?"

"I don't care what you call me," Alex said abruptly. Perhaps this wasn't going well after all.

At that, one of the people with her gave a tittering laugh. She was a young woman dressed in finery that complemented her tall, dark-haired, golden-skinned beauty. Next to her, the small, brown-haired queen looked like a badly dressed mouse. "Oh, Your Majesty," the courtier said brightly. "*This* is the royal librarian!

We've all been talking about him." She gave Alex a sneering smile. "*How* many days do you have left before you are asked to leave?"

Alex gave her a look of keen dislike. "Eleven," he answered.

"We believe it is ten," the queen corrected him.

She was right, of course.

Then the queen narrowed her eyes, studying Alex. "We are wondering where you got that coat."

Oh, the royal *we*. He'd forgotten about that. He looked down at himself. He didn't know where his pages had found the coat, but he liked it. Even though it was a little big, it made him look librarianish, he thought. But he didn't want to talk about what he was wearing.

"Never mind the coat," he said. "I need to talk to you."

"We asked you," she said, as if through gritted teeth, "a question."

"I know"—Alex gritted back at her—"that you did."

For a long moment, they exchanged glares.

Then a man stepped out from behind the beautiful courtier and cleared his throat, demanding the queen's attention.

It was *the* man, the same courtier who had, somehow, gotten into the library.

The lurker. The sneak.

Alex saw a flicker of some emotion cross the queen's face. Fear? No, it couldn't have been. Worry, maybe. Whatever it was, she controlled it immediately. "This is the new royal librarian, Merwyn Farnsworth," she said to the man. Turning to Alex, she said, "Librarian Farnsworth, this is our uncle, formerly our regent, Lord Patchedren."

Oh, so he was the queen's uncle. Formerly her *regent*. So that explained it. Her uncle had ruled the kingdom while the queen had been too young, and then she'd taken over. They probably had an . . . interesting relationship.

"We've met," Alex said, and gave her uncle the kind of edged smile that said *I don't like you and I know you don't like me, so don't even bother, all right?*

Lord Patchedren smiled right back at him, but it was a bland smile with no edge at all. "I rather suspect, my dear Kenneret," he said to the queen, "that this . . . *ahem* . . . young person has come here to beg you to give him some help. As we know, it is a job that requires a librarian of great wisdom and experience."

Which was not Alex, obviously.

Ordinarily, Alex would be more than happy to argue that point, but he wasn't stupid enough to start an argument with the queen's uncle in front of all these courtiers. Instead, he nodded. "Yes," he said to the queen. "I do need your help with something." And because her uncle and the other courtiers were watching avidly, he added, "Your Majesty."

"We are busy just now." With a hand, the queen gestured toward the lavishly dressed people around them. "Can't you ask the steward?"

"No," Alex answered. "She doesn't like me. It has to be you."

At that, the queen sighed, just the tiniest bit.

And Alex saw that he was making a mistake. He had a feeling that her uncle did this. He demanded her time and attention, whether she wanted to give it to him or not.

Well, he was sorry. But he had to do it. It was for the library. For the books.

"Look, it'll only take a moment," he said quickly. "Just two things. The first is, I need better light to work."

"Candles," she said, enunciating the word, as if he was stupid for not thinking of them before. "Surely my *steward* can give you a box of candles? It is not something that we can supply you with, at the moment."

As if she'd made a joke, her uncle and the courtiers standing around them tittered.

Alex ignored them. "Candles?" he repeated.

"Yes, of course," she said sharply.

"Candles." He shook his head. "In a *library*?" He

kept a grip on his temper. "We can't have candles. We need light-wells." *We*, he was saying. The *librarian we*— he spoke for himself, and for the books.

She was already shaking her head. "Light-wells are too expensive."

He stared at her, outraged. She wore jewels on every finger, and she thought a few light-wells would cost too much? "Candles make no sense at all," he said. "Open flame? The library is full of *books*. Paper. Lots of it. And you want me to use candles? Why don't you save some time and go burn the library down yourself?"

As he grew more furious, she seemed to grow calmer, more controlled. "You are dismissed," she said.

"What?" he asked, feeling as if he'd been slapped. "You can't dismiss me. I'm a librarian. And you gave me until the end of the month."

"From our presence," she clarified. "Not from the palace. We are not dismissing you from our service, we are telling you to leave us. Now."

"Oh," Alex said, and as much as he wanted to argue with her, he didn't want her to decide she'd better get rid of him before his trial period was over. "All right. Your Majesty." He gave an awkward bow. "Thank you for your time." He gave Lord Patchedren a sharp *stay out of my library* look, and turned to leave the garden.

"Librarian," the queen said, and he turned back.

She raised a hand, holding him in place. "Wait."

She cocked her head, studying him, and then seemed to come to a decision. "Two things," she said. "You said you had two things to speak to us about. Light sources was one. What was the other?"

Alex was impressed. She didn't miss much, did she?

He stepped closer to her, aware of how the guards at the back of the group went on high alert. "I wanted to talk to you about something strange that happened in the library," he said in a low voice, completely serious.

"Surely, my dear," her uncle put in smoothly, "this is not something that should concern you." He put his gloved fingers on her arm, as if to guide her away.

To Alex's surprise, the queen gave her uncle a polite smile. "Surely, Uncle, the queen should be concerned with everything?" And she neatly slipped her elbow out of his grip and took a step toward Alex. "We will walk with the librarian," she said, all brisk business. "Uncle, Lady Arriss, my lords and ladies, you may continue without us."

More murmuring from the courtiers, as Lady Arriss said something rude, mimicking Alex's northern accent. Led by Lord Patchedren, the rest of the group laughed mockingly as they moved off in a bejeweled, laced, sneering group.

Alex glared after them. "Are you always surrounded

by people you don't like?" he asked the queen.

"What makes you think we do not like them?" she responded.

"Because they're awful," Alex said. "Especially that slippery uncle of yours."

"Our uncle," the queen said sharply, "not only faithfully served us as regent for ten years, but has always taken most tender care of us."

"Oh, *sure* he has," Alex muttered.

Ignoring his comment, Queen Kenneret nodded at the guards, who followed at a distance while she and Alex walked side by side down a path between two high hedges. Without speaking, they turned a corner into an open area of the garden. Leaving the guards at the edge of this area, Alex and the queen walked along the gravel path that wound between low rosebushes and still ponds that reflected the gray sky. In this part of the garden, they weren't protected from the chilly wind. Winter was definitely on its way. The queen was wearing a stiffly formal green brocade dress with a high lace collar and skirts that made her seem almost as wide as she was tall. A fur cape had been tossed over her shoulders, but her ears looked red with cold. Alex was glad for the woolly hat his pages had brought him. Queens, he figured, didn't get to wear hats with pompons on them. Only cold golden crowns.

He shoved his hands deep into his coat pockets to keep them warm, and tried to think of what he was going to tell the queen. She expected him to fail. He knew it. She thought the library wasn't important. But now that he'd found the book with the symbol burned into it, he knew that he couldn't face what he was dealing with alone, even though he had his pages to help him. He needed an ally, and he liked her best of all the people he'd met since he'd left home.

"The library," the queen said, as they walked along, "does not usually take up so much of our time."

"Well, it should," Alex answered.

"Why?" she asked. She sounded genuinely interested.

"You've got something weird going on here," Alex answered. "The library's been neglected, that's part of it. Given enough time, I can deal with that." He looked around, and then led her to an empty vegetable bed. "But there's something else." Crouching, he smoothed out the dirt with his hands. "Maybe I'd better not draw it," he muttered to himself. Then he shrugged. It couldn't do any harm out here. With a glance over his shoulder at the guards—they were too far away to see what he was doing—he traced his finger through the dirt, drawing the symbol he'd seen on the books that had attacked him and his master. Still crouching, he looked up at her. "Have you ever seen this before?"

She leaned closer to see. "No," she answered. "What is it?"

He studied the symbol. "I don't know."

"Is it important?"

He got to his feet, dusting his hands off on the front of his coat. Was it important? What sort of question was that? "It's the library we're talking about. Of course it's important," he told her. "I think it might be very dangerous. A book with this mark on it attacked me."

She led him to a marble bench, where she sat, her back absolutely straight. She probably couldn't slouch; the dress wouldn't let her. "Dangerous," she repeated. "Books are inanimate objects. They don't *attack* people."

He took four steps away from her to keep control of his temper, and then paced back. "Books can kill. I think they *have* killed."

She blinked, and a frown gathered between her arched eyebrows. "The books in the royal library?"

"Some of them, yes." He paced again, with his hands clasped behind his back. She didn't believe him. She'd never seen a book that did anything but sit on a shelf. He wasn't sure what to do next. "Can I have more time?" he attempted.

She got to her feet and smoothed her skirts. "No. You were given until the end of the month. After that, your performance will be evaluated."

He kicked a piece of gravel and bit back a curse. "Well, give me a couple of assistants, then."

"No," she said in what he was already thinking of as her *queenly* voice. "We are curious. Why a librarian?"

"What do you mean?" he asked.

"Why did you choose to become a librarian?" she asked.

He shrugged and kicked another piece of gravel. It bounced across the path and fell into one of the pools with a *plonk*. This whole thing was hopeless. The library would still be a mess at the end of the month. It looked worse than before he'd started, because to get it organized he'd pulled hundreds—no, *thousands*—of books off the shelves, and they were in piles everywhere. To a non-librarian it would look like a total disaster. *And* when the book had attacked him, he had realized that the approach he'd been using was wrong. He'd thought that cataloging the books would help to settle them, but clearly that wasn't working. He needed to start all over again. But as soon as the month ended he'd be tossed out of the palace just as winter was starting. He had nowhere else to go, and he wasn't much interested in freezing to death. Blast it, he'd probably have to go *home*, which was the last place he wanted to be, even though he missed . . . certain people . . . with an ache that had settled into his very bones. And the royal library would become even more dangerous after he left.

"I just wondered," he heard her murmur, "why someone like you would choose to be a librarian."

Alex's head whipped up, and he stared at her. She had said *I*. Not the royal *we*. "I'm just like you," he said, on impulse.

"We rather think that you are nothing like us," she said, all frosty distance again.

"Yes, I am," he said, growing more certain. "I didn't choose to be a librarian. My father hates it. He wants me to . . ." He shook his head. "Never mind. A librarian is what I am. It's the same for you." He pointed at her. "You didn't choose to be queen. It's not easy, and I think there are people who want you to fail at it." Her uncle, he guessed. "But a queen is what you are."

She stared at him for a long, silent moment. A flush crept up her face, and her mouth trembled. Then she took a steadying breath and lifted her chin. "It does sound as if you have a lot of work to do before the end of the month, Librarian Farnsworth." She must have made some kind of gesture, because the guards were coming toward them, weaving between the vegetable beds and statuary. "And there's one more thing," she added, before he could leave.

"Yes?" he asked. "Your Majesty?"

"You said before that our steward does not like you."

"That's right," Alex confirmed.

Completely in control of herself again, she gave him an edged smile. "Well, we do not like you either."

Alex shrugged and then—he couldn't help it—he grinned at her, not librarian to queen, but boy to girl not much older than he was. "That's all right," he said, and felt a flash of triumph when he saw her blink in surprise. "As far as I know, nobody likes me."

And before she could say anything else, he whirled and hurried out of the garden and up the stairs. The very second the palace door had closed behind him, he summoned two of his pages.

Librarian, they wrote as they hovered before him only barely visible, as if they didn't like being seen outside the library. *What do you command?*

The pages, he figured, had stolen the coat he was wearing from somewhere. The queen had clearly recognized it. So they were thieves. That was not an entirely bad thing.

"Pages," he ordered, "find me light-wells. Take them from anywhere in the palace. Steal them if you have to, and bring them to the library."

12

I am a queen, Kenneret told herself. She stood before the tall mirror in the royal attiring room and inspected herself from the top of her head to the tips of the embroidered shoes that peeked from under her wide skirts. Her ladies-in-waiting had dressed her in pink satin today, a dress covered with flounces and frills. She looked, she thought, like a cupcake. With lace frosting.

We are the queen.

She was the queen, and yet her uncle had scolded her after she'd left him in the garden to talk to the librarian.

Well, not *scolded,* exactly. Uncle Patch would never

mar his face with a frown. But he'd reminded her in his most reasonable voice how important it was to *cultivate relationships* with the nobles and courtiers who flocked to the Winter Palace when the harvest was in. *You have to make yourself popular,* he advised. *You have to make them like you.* And then he'd looked grave. *I am very much afraid, my dear, that you have not yet shown them your likable side.*

She gave a little snort. The librarian clearly never worried about showing *his* likable side.

While she had to keep proving herself, over and over, every day. And it was only getting worse. There were snide comments that seemed to mean one thing on the surface, and meant something completely different once she'd thought about it. People wanted things from her, constantly. Her orders were somehow misinterpreted, almost as if somebody was secretly, insidiously sabotaging her, trying to make her look bad. She worked hard, late into the night, and there was always, always something she'd neglected to do.

She did not have time to deal with the royal library.

Or the royal librarian.

He was a very strange boy.

All the courtiers and nobles—they saw her as somebody who could get them what they wanted, which was power. But they never came right out and asked for anything. It was all subtle, suggested, implied. Whisperings. Secrets and intrigue. The librarian was different. He didn't care what anyone thought of him. He knew what he wanted and he came right out and asked for it. And if he wasn't given what he needed—what the library needed—he went out and got it.

Two days ago, the steward had come to her with complaints that the librarian had somehow stolen every unsecured light-well in the palace.

She needed to be that kind of queen.

Carefully she unpinned the lace fichu around her neck and stripped the jeweled rings from her fingers. The rings had hidden the calluses on her hands, but she couldn't worry about that now.

"Your Majesty!" protested one of her ladies-in-waiting, Lady Arriss. When she had picked out the pink dress, she had held it out to Kenneret with a sly smile. Tall, graceful Arriss, of course, would look stunningly beautiful in such a dress, and the lady-in-waiting clearly knew that the same dress would make Kenneret look ridiculous.

Ignoring her, Kenneret kicked off the embroidered slippers and stepped into her closet, where she found the dresses she'd worn before she'd been crowned queen. With quick fingers, she unlaced the stiff bodice of the pink cupcake dress and slipped it off, leaving it in a pink heap on the floor.

The three ladies-in-waiting clustered at the door of the closet, protesting as Kenneret put on a simple sky-blue gown made of the softest lambswool, with a plain collar secured by a flat, gold pin that her mother had worn when she had been queen. A carefully chosen detail. This gown had pearly buttons up the front, ones she could do up herself. She put on fleece-lined boots with just a bit of heel, to give herself some more height. Ready, she went to the mirror, where she straightened and took a deep breath. There. Much better. She looked plain and tidy, and she felt like herself.

It was stupid to think that simply changing her clothes would change . . . oh, how people like Lady Arriss spoke to her, or treated her, but the fashions of the Winter Palace made her look like a ridiculous mushroom, she knew it, and wearing what she actually wanted to was a start. She would not listen to whispers and lace and jewels and flounces and lies. Like the librarian, she would ask for what she wanted, and she would get it, too.

Carefully she set the gold circlet on her head, stuck in a few pins to hold it there, and pushed past her ladies. She was sure she heard a snigger as she went out of the attiring room.

Her steward was waiting for her in the anteroom.

"Your Majesty," Dorriss said with a smooth bow. "Your brother has arrived. He awaits you in the blue salon."

Kenneret felt her heart leap. Charlie had been scheduled to arrive four days ago. Who knew what he'd been up to, to make him so late. "Have tea and toast sent up," she ordered. "We will meet him there." She stepped toward the door, then stopped. "And inform Lady Arriss that we no longer require her service." She heard a gasp from the ladies behind her.

Her uncle would have something to say about it, but she would hold firm. The librarian was right. These people *were* awful. And she was queen. She didn't have to put up with them if she didn't want to. She didn't have to be *likable* or *nice*. She had to be good at trade negotiations and setting tax rates and dealing with the farmers' guild.

Feeling lighter of heart than she had in a long time, she strode through the hallways, past bowing and curtseying servants and nobles, and the diplomatic delegation from the north, where a conflict with their warlike Greyling neighbors was brewing again.

She went straight to the blue salon, where she found her brother, Charlie, sprawled on a silk sofa with his boots propped on a priceless table. "Hullo, Kennie," he said, getting to his feet.

"Charlie," she said as they gave each other the traditional greeting, a kiss on each cheek. Then she held him at arm's length, inspecting him.

He was her younger brother, but he was taller than she was by five inches. No, six—he'd grown since the summer. Like her, he had a snub nose and skin that tanned easily in the summer and paled to a sort of sallow olive in the winter, and dark brown hair, but his had a bit of curl in it that made him look dashing, even though he was only fourteen. He was big—he had big hands and big feet, and one day, when he grew into them, he would be a very large, intimidating man.

But for now he was just awkward, and quite astonishingly clumsy, as if furniture and sharp corners leaped out to make him trip or bump his shins, or drop whatever he was carrying. His booted feet, she noticed, had left scratches on the surface of the table he'd propped them on.

"Here," he said, holding out a grubby letter and then flopping down on the sofa again.

She sat primly on a chair.

The letter was from the headmaster at his school,

Starkcliffe. "Oh, Charlie," she murmured as she read. "Oh, *Charlie*." She looked up at him. "Have you read this?"

"No," he said sullenly, staring at the toes of his boots.

"Disruptive in class," she read aloud. "Failure in every subject. Fights. No friends. Bullying! Charlie, you're a prince! You can't be a bully!"

He shifted uncomfortably. "I know. I'm supposed to be like *you*. Always setting a good example."

She sighed. "Have you talked to Uncle Patch yet?"

He swallowed and shook his head. "No." He shot her a nervous glance. "D'you think he'll be angry, Kennie?"

"I think it's very likely," she answered, folding the headmaster's letter. Not that Uncle Patch would show it. He never did. But both she and her brother knew very well that their uncle felt much more than he showed.

Charlie was a prince, but unless something dire happened to her, he would never be king. He hated school, and always had. His life had no purpose. He tried to hide it, but with her keen eye for details, she could see signs that he wasn't just a troublemaker, he was deeply unhappy. What was she going to *do* with him?

And then she had a quite brilliant idea.

13

Alex woke up on the ratty velvet couch in his office. His nose was cold. The rest of him was warm. During the night, his pages had put an extra blanket over him, and then they'd added more layers—another blanket, a pile of cleaning rags, a towel that smelled like it had been used to rub down a horse, and a beautifully embroidered curtain. He didn't want to crawl out from under it all. His office was freezing. So was the library. A few days ago he'd sent a note to the steward about getting heat to this part of the palace, but she'd written back that the queen had ordered that the heat should be cut off.

He'd have to ask Her Royal Majesty about it.

Not that it mattered that much. He'd been working hard, long hours, but he didn't have many days left to figure out why the books were waking up, and why some of them were being marked by that symbol and turned into dangerous traps. He only had until the end of the month.

And then, disaster.

Carefully he snaked an arm out from under his pile of blankets and things, grabbed his coat, pulled it into his warm nest, and wrestled himself into it. As soon as he did, a page drifted in and set a steaming cup on his desk.

Flinging back the blankets and covers, Alex shivered into his scuffed shoes, pulled on his woolly hat, and then went to sit at his desk, where he cradled his hands around the teacup, breathing in the steam.

His pa liked a hot cup of tea in the morning, too.

And followed it with a brisk set of sword drills and, if the weather was less abysmally foul than usual, a ten-mile run, along with a troop of men-at-arms, some of whom were women-at-arms. As a refresher, they'd all strip down and race into the lake, which was freezing even during the summer, swim for a bit, and *then* have breakfast.

Alex shivered just thinking about it.

Just as he was looking about for a book to read as he drank his tea, a page drifted past his left shoulder and brushed his cheek, a comforting touch. A moment later, a letter dropped onto the desk in front of him.

With chilled fingers, Alex turned it over and read the envelope.

It was addressed to the former royal librarian, Maeviss Clark—the one who had died here.

He shook his head, trying to ignore the foreboding thought that if he wasn't careful, *he* could die here, too.

Opening the letter, Alex saw that it was from the librarian—ancient, of course—at a library in Far Wrothing.

My dearest Maeviss,

I write to you, my dear friend, with a professional concern, which is that the library here has been behaving most peculiarly. As you know, I have looked after the books here with utmost care and concern for many years. But then I found a book with a certain symbol on its cover that I will not reproduce here.

Suspecting what it might be, I have not opened this book, but have instead sequestered it in a locked room. Despite my precautions, I fear it is affecting the other books. They are restless and—I think quite possibly they are frightened. There have been some rather strange occurrences.

My friend, I rather fear that the presence of this marked book means that one of the L.B.s is hidden here in my library, though I have not yet been able to find it. I have always assumed that we dealt with the L.B.s long ago—sixty years, by my count. It terrifies me to think that, after all this time, we may have failed, after all.

Please advise me soonest as to what I should do.

Your colleague,

Jackys Hockett

"Pen," Alex muttered, opening a desk drawer and searching through it. He set out paper, took up the pen that one of his pages brought him, and found that the ink was almost frozen in its bottle. After stirring it up, he began writing a letter to Librarian Hockett, asking her what she meant by *L.B.*s, and why it or they or whatever it was had been hidden in her library. There were other secrets in this letter, too. What, *exactly*, had happened sixty years ago? He needed answers! He was just about to sign his letter *Merwyn Farnsworth* when a thought hit him like a brick falling on his head.

He sat up straight. A bead of ink gathered at the tip of his pen and fell, *splat*, in the middle of the letter.

The Far Wrothing librarian. She could be the target of this marked book—she might be killed by it, just as his master had been, and just like the royal librarian. She was in danger, terrible danger.

Quickly Alex crumpled up the letter he'd been writing, tossed it aside, and pulled out a clean piece of paper.

Librarian Hockett,

he wrote.

*You must immediately lock the marked book
in a box and send it to me, and absolutely do
not open it.*

After thinking for a moment, he added:

*I regret to tell you that your friend Maeviss
Clark, the former royal librarian, has died.
I think it very likely that one of the marked
books killed her. Do not underestimate your own
danger.*

Then he signed it:

Merwyn Farnsworth

And then he added a postscript.

*P.S. Write out whatever you know about the
L.B.s and what happened sixty years ago and
send it to me at once.*

Hockett had written that *the books are frightened.*
The books here were frightened, too—it explained
their behavior, all the flying around, the barricading, the flinging from shelves, the rattling of chains.
The fact that the same sort of thing was happening in
other libraries meant the problem was bigger than he
thought, something to do with these *L.B.*s, whatever

they were, and with librarian secrets. He needed to figure it out as soon as he possibly could.

And he had no *time*. Only a few days, that was it.

Alex folded his letter, stuffed it into an envelope, and jumped to his feet. He'd take it to the steward himself. After carefully locking the library door behind him, he made his way through the dusty hallways of the palace to the steward's office.

She was there, behind her desk, working. As he entered, she looked up and gave him one of her disapproving looks.

"Yeah, I know," he said. "You don't like me. The feeling is mutual, all right?"

"It does not matter whether I like you or not, Librarian," she said, putting down her pen. "I do not trust you—that is what counts."

"You can trust me to do what's best for the library," he said.

She got to her feet. "And you can trust me to do what is right for the queen. Always." The truth of that shone in her dark eyes.

And Alex understood. They both served something bigger than they were. With a nod, he held out the letter. "This has to go today by the fastest means possible," he ordered.

Raising her eyebrows, the steward took the letter.

"It's a matter of life and death," he added.

"Very well," she said. "It will go today."

"Good. Thank you." And with that, he left. She was loyal, he had to admit, and she was good at her job. She'd see the letter got to the librarian at Far Wrothing. He headed back to the library.

He was walking head down, thinking, and had just turned the corner and into the hallway that led to the library door, when he nearly ran into someone.

It was the queen's uncle, Lord Patchedren. "Ah, Librarian *Farnsworth*," he said, with just a bit of an emphasis to show that he knew Alex wasn't who he said he was. He smiled and slipped a book into the pocket of his laced silk coat. He'd been coming from the library, even though the door was locked. More of his sneaking around.

"You're searching for something," Alex realized suddenly.

"*Am* I?" Lord Patch asked.

"In the library," Alex went on.

"Now what would I be looking for in a library?" Lord Patch said, and he smiled faintly, as if he and Alex were sharing a joke.

One that wasn't funny. "A book," Alex said grimly.

"You're looking for a book."

Still smiling, Lord Patch said, "You have no idea what you're dealing with, do you?"

"I know enough to be sure that you shouldn't be in there." Alex pointed down the hallway at the library door.

"Oh, *dear* boy." Lord Patch shook his head, mock-sorrowfully.

"Don't *dear boy* me," Alex snapped.

Lord Patch looked Alex over from head to toe. And then he looked past Alex's shoulder and the faintest of frown lines appeared between his invisible eyebrows.

Alex knew what he'd seen. "Yes, I have pages now," he said. "Lots of them. I am a librarian."

"So you are," Lord Patch murmured. "So you are." Then he gave a tiny nod, as if he'd decided something. "You can feel no personal loyalty to the queen," Patch said in a low voice. "And I understand the library in a way that she cannot. Perhaps you might consider working for me."

When he thought about this offer later, Alex realized that he should have pretended to take it so he could figure out what the queen's uncle was up to. But in the moment, all he felt was outrage. "Not likely," he snapped. "Why would I want to work for you when I don't like you *or* trust you?"

Lord Patch's dark eyes hardened. "You are in far more danger than you realize."

"Is that a threat?" Alex reached for the sword at his waist—except that he wasn't wearing a sword, *hadn't* worn a sword since he'd left home.

Lord Patch saw the gesture and knew what it meant. "Not a threat, no," he said, and then gave his toothless smile that had no warmth in it at all. "Not a threat from me, at any rate. A warning." Smoothly he stepped around Alex. "Be careful, Librarian. If you can." And with that, he strode down the hallway.

Alex frowned, watching him go. He hadn't told anyone about the book that had attacked him, or about the letter from Librarian Hockett. Somehow Lord Patch knew more than he did about what was really going on in the library.

The thought rankled.

And Patch was clearly up to something. He *seemed* supportive of Queen Kenneret, but what if he wasn't really?

Shaking his head, he went down the hallway to the library door, which was locked, of course. He went in and locked it behind him. He couldn't worry about the queen and her uncle and politics. He had an entire unsettled library to deal with.

As he crossed the big main room, heading to his office, his pages trailed behind him like a flock of fluttering birds. "We've got a lot of work to do," he told them, setting his bunch of keys on his desk. The letter from Librarian Hockett had made him realize what his new approach to the problem of the marked books would be. Instead of trying to catalog books that were too frightened to stay organized, he would find the thing that was frightening them. He would search the library for books with the symbol on their covers. Those marked books were traps laid for an unsuspecting librarian, which he was not. He was suspecting now, that was for sure. He would pick up every book as if it were a bomb ready to go off.

Then one of his pages delivered another letter, just a single piece of paper, but it was direly gilded.

To: Merwyn "Alex" Farnsworth, Royal Librarian

Librarian Farnsworth,

We summon you to our presence in the gold receiving room during the third hour past noon. You will report to us your progress in organizing the books in the royal library.

Signed,

H.R.M. Queen Kenneret III

Alex stared at the note, then read it again. He had three days to figure out what was going on in the library before the queen kicked him out. He didn't have time for this. Quickly he scrawled a response.

Can't. Too busy.
—A.

"Page!" he called. One of his pages appeared at his shoulder. Alex held up the note. "Deliver this to the queen."

The page wafted away, bringing the note with it.

Half an hour later, Alex was standing in a remote chamber of the library, one hacked out of the cliff, trying to figure out where a persistent humming sound was coming from. There must be a room full of music books around here somewhere, but he couldn't find it. It wasn't really a hum they were making. More of a low chanting sound. It was starting to get on his nerves.

Then the page he'd sent off before reappeared and dropped the same scrap of paper on the floor at his feet.

On the back of his note, the queen had written her response.

Alex, that's an order. —Q. K.

"All right, all right," he muttered. He would just get these music books tracked down and check them for the thing that was making them so nervously noisy—he feared one of them was marked with that mysterious symbol—and then he would go see what the queen wanted.

Later—*much* later—he woke up suddenly as the door of the library slammed.

Sitting up, he rubbed his eyes. He had fallen asleep at one of the long tables in the big main room. Books were piled all around him. The card catalogs were open, and cards were scattered everywhere. It *looked* random and disorganized, but he had a system for his searching for the marked books. It would look even worse before it got better.

Had he heard the door slam? It was late. Very late. The main room was cavernous and dark, and chilly. He could almost see his breath, it was so cold. The books were silent.

A flare of light came from the direction of the door.

A boy about his own age, broad-shouldered and slouchy, with a clump of wavy brown hair shaved on the sides like a soldier in training, stood at the edge of the big main room looking around. He held a candelabra—four candles all lit up and burning.

Alex shot to his feet. *Candles!* In *his* library!

"Ah," the other boy said, in a supercilious voice. "You, boy. I am looking for somebody called Farnsworth."

"Put those candles out," Alex ordered.

The other boy looked at the candelabra in his fist, then he reached out to set it on the nearest table—and missed.

"Gah!" Alex cried, and leaped to stamp on the flames as the candles scattered over the floor.

In the sudden dimness, the other boy looked hulking. Alex was nearly the same height, but the other boy was a lot bigger. Still, Alex stepped closer and poked him in the chest. "How did you get into my library?"

A big fist seized Alex's finger and held it. "*Your* library?"

"I," Alex gritted out, pulling his hand away, "am the royal librarian."

"But you're a kid," the boy protested.

"Nevertheless," Alex said. "Now, tell me how you got in here."

The pages were bringing light-wells, so he could see the other boy better.

And the boy could see him. He was examining Alex, from head to foot. "You're wearing my old coat," he said slowly. "Kennie said I'd know Farnsworth because he had something of mine."

Alex opened his mouth, and then closed it again. *Kennie?* As in *Her Royal Majesty Queen Kenneret?* Who *was* this lout?

"The steward gave me a key." The boy held up a key to the library door, then shoved it into his pocket. "And Kennie gave me a note to give to you." He held out a folded piece of paper.

When Alex opened it, he saw the gilded crest.

Librarian Farnsworth—
This is the new assistant you requested. Keep him occupied and out of trouble.
—Q. Kenneret III

Alex crumpled the letter and tossed it over his shoulder. "You're her brother, aren't you?"

"Yep," the boy said. "You can call me *Prince Charleren*, or *Your Highness.*" He looked around the room. With a faintly worried tone in his voice, he said, "Lots of books you've got here."

"Because it's a *library*," Alex said through gritted teeth. He clenched his fists and glared at the other boy, who stared blankly back at him. Oh, the queen was good at getting what she wanted. Clearly this lout of a brother needed a babysitter, and she'd decided that she could get Alex to do it.

Well, blast it all to pieces. She was right. He needed the help, no matter what the source.

📖

The next morning, Prince Charleren was supposed to start working as Alex's assistant.

Alex, who had been up since before dawn, was instructing his pages to search for the charred symbol in a room full of poetry books that kept shifting from one shelf to another. He ignored the other boy as he unlocked the door and came louting into the library an hour late.

"Try the catwalk off the fifth-level balcony," Alex was saying to one of his pages. "Aren't there a few doors around there that we haven't opened yet?"

The page fluttered as the prince approached, then flitted off to do Alex's bidding.

"Why's it so cold in here?" Charleren asked.

Alex, who was wearing his woolly hat, half-fingered gloves, a warm scarf, and the prince's old coat, was not going to make idle chat with this idle prince. "Go make yourself useful," he told the other boy.

"What should I do?" Charleren asked.

Alex glanced around the big room, looking for

inspiration. "Dust. Go and dust the woodwork on the balconies."

"I don't *dust*," the prince said, offended.

"Fine," Alex said, going back to the papers on his table. He was trying to put together a map of the library so he could mark off the rooms he had searched. "Then I don't care what you do. Just don't talk to me while you do it."

With a shrug, the prince shoved his hands in his pockets and headed for the windows, scuffing straight through ten piles of carefully organized and alphabetized book cards.

"Gah!" Alex shouted, his voice echoing in the huge room. "Stop!"

The prince turned, messing up the cards even more. "What?"

"Don't move," Alex ordered. The cards had taken him *hours* to organize. "Just—" He looked around. "Go sit over there." He pointed at a chair at a long reading table.

Lifting his big feet carefully, the prince crossed the room and slouched into a chair.

Alex went back to work, reading over his hand-drawn map. He was starting to realize that there were sections of the library that he hadn't even found yet. Hidden doors, he guessed. Passages behind bookcases. Maybe tunnels under the main room. The marked books—the *traps*—could be hiding in any of those places.

"Starkcliffe," the prince said, interrupting him.

Alex looked up. The other boy had leaned back in his chair and propped his boots on the table, and was staring up at the ceiling. "What?" Alex asked.

The prince glanced at him, then back up. "They send me to this military academy called Starkcliffe. Stark. Cliff. Can you even imagine?"

Yes, Alex could imagine it very well. His own father had gone to school there, and had told him terrifying stories about it. "Why didn't you run away?" he found himself asking.

"I *have*," the prince answered. "They always send me back. Our uncle doesn't want me around until I *grow out of it*, whatever that means."

Alex felt a certain amount of sympathy for the other boy. Still, he didn't want Charleren messing around with his books.

"He looks at me like I'm stupid," the prince went on. Then he added, in a quieter voice, as if he was trying to convince himself, "I'm not stupid."

Alex didn't comment. From all he'd seen so far, the prince was, in fact, a royally colossal idiot. But he could do *something*. With his pages' eager help, he quickly gathered the cards that the prince had disarranged.

"Here," he said, dumping them on the table before the other boy. "Put these into alphabetical order by title." Before the prince could protest, Alex pointed toward the fifth level. "I'll be up there trying to find a missing room. Have it done before I get back."

Later, after spending two hours crawling through an icy-cold tunnel that turned out to lead nowhere, Alex came back into the main room of the library to find Prince Charleren still sitting where Alex had left him, still staring at the ceiling, the cards a jumbled mess on the table before him.

Alex felt his temper begin to fray. "So, Lump," he said acidly. "Got a lot done while I was gone?"

"That's *Your Highness* to you," the prince said sullenly.

The tunnel's icy dampness had left Alex shivering, his pages had forgotten to bring him lunch, and he'd been too busy to remember it until now. And he only had two days left. He didn't have time for this. He glared at the other boy. "*Your Lumpness*, you mean," Alex spat.

"How dare you?" The prince got to his feet so suddenly that his chair tipped over behind him, clattering on the stone floor. "I will tell the queen about this disrespect."

"Go ahead," Alex shot back. He liked feeling angry.

His temper warmed him right up. "But it's clear that she already knows that you're useless."

The prince went very pale. He swallowed once, and then choked out a curse. "I'm not—not *useless*."

"Obviously you are," Alex said, relentless. "Why else would your sister try dumping you on me?"

"You want to see how useless I am, Librarian?" Charleren stood with his hands clenched into fists.

"You've already demonstrated that," Alex answered, pointing at the jumble of book cards still scattered on the table. "You won't dust or sweep. You won't help put things in order. You've barely even looked at the books. What are you even doing here? Hmm? Lump?"

Prince Charleren spoke through stiff lips, as if the words were being wrenched out of him. "You—you need to be taught a lesson, and I'm the one who's going to teach it to you." He pointed at the door to the library. "Practice hall in ten minutes. Swords. With—with edges on them!"

"What are you even talking about?" Alex scoffed.

The prince glared furiously at him, but when he answered, his voice had a note of triumph. "I'm challenging you to a duel, *Librarian*. You're going to regret calling me *useless* for the rest of your entire extremely short life!"

14

Queens did not run.

Kenneret could, however, make her legs move very quickly under her woolen skirt and layers of petticoats. It *looked* like a glide, but it was fast.

A courtier had burst into her office, interrupting a meeting with her team of diplomats who were working on the Greyling situation. "Your Majesty!" he gasped, bowing, and then bowing again. "His Royal Highness Prince Charleren is about to fight a duel with the royal librarian."

She dropped everything and hurried to the practice hall, with the steward, the puffing courtier, and three footmen trailing behind her. She didn't *like* the librarian, exactly, but she didn't want him to get hurt, either, and Charlie had been trained at Starkcliffe, after all.

When she arrived at the practice hall, she was not at all surprised to find that half the royal court, including her uncle, was there before her. During the long, humid summers, the people of Aethel farmed, growing abundant vegetables and wheat in the kingdom's rich dirt. During the short, bitterly cold winters, they studied the sword and other weapons. The courtiers who came to spend the winter at the palace *loved* duels. They were chattering with excitement. As Kenneret came up, the sword master caught her eye and gave her a nod, which she returned. She knew him well, of course. Then two courtiers, girls her own age, curtseyed and stepped aside to give her room at the front.

Both girls, she noticed, were wearing simple woolen gowns like her own practical dress, instead of the fancily flounced lace and silk of the rest of the court.

Kenneret smiled at them, and they smiled shyly back.

She knew what their plain dresses meant, and it made her heart warm toward them. It meant she wasn't alone. She had allies. Or, at the very least, people who didn't dislike her simply because she had power and they did not.

The practice hall was a huge room with a rear wall of hewn stone and a row of windows opposite it. Racks of weapons took up the rest of the wall space, along with padded vests, and targets, and a slate board with chalk for keeping track of the practice schedule.

Her brother was doing stretching exercises, jumping up and down to loosen his muscles. From the look on his face, Kenneret could see that he was furious. But there was something else, too, something that seemed almost desperate.

She glided—quickly—up to him. "Charlie, *what* is going on?"

He hooked his arm behind his head and stretched his neck. "I'm going to poke a lot of holes in the royal librarian, that's what."

"Why?" she demanded. "What did he do?"

"He insulted me," Charlie answered.

Well, that she could believe. "But you can't *kill* him for it," she protested.

"Yes, I can," he said, and suddenly his voice sounded miserable. *Something* was going on.

"Practice swords," she said gently.

Charlie swung around to face her. For a moment she thought he was going to protest, and then he nodded. "All right." He started unbuttoning his coat.

Kenneret glanced across the room to where the

librarian was standing by himself, arms crossed, looking annoyed. And also unlikely to withstand Charlie's assault for very long. She saw one of the weapons masters offer him a selection of practice swords; he shrugged and picked one, almost at random.

"Try not to hurt him too badly," she said to her brother.

He gave her a sudden, rather wolfish grin. "I'll try." He held out his coat, and she took it; then, before he could pull away, she grasped his hand.

Turning her brother's big hand in her own, while he stood looking down at her, she traced the fine white scars on the backs of his knuckles. "Charlie," she said softly, realizing that the fight might not be as unbalanced as she expected, "the librarian has scars like this on his hands."

"From training with the sword?" he asked, tugging his hand away. Then he snorted. "I doubt it. They're probably from paper cuts."

The sword master was approaching with a selection of practice blades.

"Well, be careful," Kenneret advised.

Charlie gave her an exasperated look. "Kennie, that is *not* what you say to somebody about to fight a duel."

It was practice swords, after all, and not edged steel. "Fight well, then," she told him, and he carefully chose a practice sword, then went to meet the librarian in the center of the room.

Kenneret rejoined the court, still holding Charlie's coat. Behind her, two nobles were taking bets on how many blows the prince would land before the librarian gave up.

Her uncle slid into a spot beside her. "Is it wise, Kenneret, allowing this?" he whispered into her ear.

She glanced over at him. Gorgeously dressed, as usual. His signature yellow silk and seed pearls. He was watching keenly as Charlie and the librarian stood listening to the rules being laid out by the sword master. She saw Charlie say something as the librarian shrugged, a response that seemed to make Charlie even more angry.

"I'm not going to stop it now," she told her uncle.

"The librarian has already proven to be disrespectful," her uncle went on. "And now this—fighting a duel with your brother. You will certainly have to order him to leave."

"He only has two days left before he leaves anyway," Kenneret answered.

She might have said more, except that Charlie and the librarian were lining up. The sword master spoke a word, stepped back, and the fight began.

A moment later, it ended.

There was a flash of blades, a yell from Charlie, and her brother's sword landed on the stone floor with a clatter.

Alex stood opposite him, still holding his own sword. "There," he said, looking almost bored. "Are we done?"

Charlie stood staring at him, his arms hanging loosely at his sides. Then he bent and snatched up his sword. "No!" He lunged at the librarian.

There was another flurry of bladework, shouts of excitement from the onlookers, and this time Charlie's sword went skidding across the floor and a fountain of blood erupted from his nose.

As Charlie sopped up the blood with the sleeve of his shirt, Kenneret broke away from the courtiers and her uncle and went to join him.

The librarian gave her a defiant look, as if he thought he was about to be dismissed.

Which he was.

Until she noticed that her brother's eyes were sparkling with excitement.

"You're . . . you're ab-abazing," Charlie said to him through a nose full of blood. "Bagnificent. Where did you learn to fight like that?"

The librarian shrugged and stayed stubbornly silent.

Charlie turned to her. "Kennie, let hib stay, just so he teaches be the sword every day."

Alex glared at him. "I'm a librarian, not a sword master."

"All right, all right," Charlie bubbled. He swiped at his bloody nose again. "I'll sweep and dust and whaddever you say, just teach be once a week."

The librarian rolled his eyes and then stepped closer to Kenneret and spoke in a low voice, so only she and Charlie could hear him. "You gave me your brother as an assistant, Your Majesty," he said. "Did you realize that he . . ." He glanced aside at Charlie. "Is it all right if I tell her?"

"You guessed?" he asked.

"I'm not an idiot," Alex answered. "It was obvious once I thought about it."

"Thed yes," Charlie said, still dabbing at his nose. "Tell her."

The librarian caught Kenneret's eye and nodded at her brother. "He doesn't know how to read."

"What?" Kenneret exclaimed, and then lowered her voice again. "Of course Charlie knows how to read. How dare you suggest—" But then she realized that Charlie was nodding his head vigorously. Drops of blood from his nose spattered on the stone floor at his feet. "Really, you don't?" she asked him.

He snuffled up some blood and then swallowed. "I really don't, Kennie," he said thickly. "I've tried and tried, and I just can't. The words crawl around too much. I wanted to tell you but I couldn't. Don't tell Uncle Patch."

No wonder he'd looked so desperate and unhappy; no wonder he'd kept getting himself tossed out of school. *Oh, Charlie*, she wanted to say. *I'm sorry*.

But the librarian was standing right there, gazing speculatively at her brother.

"What?" Kenneret prompted.

"I think..." the librarian began, and then shrugged. "Given what's been happening with the books, having an assistant who can't read..." He gave a decided nod. "He might be very, very useful."

To her astonishment, her brother let out a crack of laughter. "Useful!" he shouted, and gave the librarian a slap on the shoulder that made the other boy stagger a few steps.

"Ow," complained the librarian, rubbing his shoulder, but grinning at Charlie, who smiled with bloody teeth back at him.

Boys. She would never understand them.

And then Uncle Patch broke into their little circle. "Most impressively done, Librarian Farnsworth. It seems you have been trained in the sword."

Kenneret was interested to note that the librarian's face, which had been lit up with happiness, went suddenly still and watchful. "Yes," he answered.

"And now you have taken on my nephew as your assistant," Uncle Patch said smoothly. "Yet you have only two more days before you are dismissed, isn't that right?"

"Yes," Alex said. "That's right." He glanced toward the door of the practice room, as if planning his escape. "It means I don't have time to stand around talking to any of you." Ignoring Uncle Patch's look of mild surprise, he held out his sword to Charlie. "Library. First thing in the morning. We have a lot to do and not much time to do it in, so don't be late."

As Charlie took the sword, the librarian turned and left the practice room—in a hurry, without looking back.

Her uncle gazed after him. "I am worried about that boy," he said, in a voice dripping with concern.

"Are you?" Kenneret asked. Her uncle didn't often show the world anything but a smoothly smiling face. His worry must be real.

"I have had reports," he said. "I have been told that he barely stops working to eat or sleep. And yet the library, I hear, is a complete disaster." He pasted on a bland smile and then took Kenneret's hand to lead her out of the practice hall. "Clearly, my dear Kenneret, Alex *Farnsworth* is incompetent. The library is too much for him to manage properly. You will simply have to insist that he leaves when his trial period is over."

"Hmm," Kenneret said, not exactly agreeing. It was odd, she thought, that her uncle was so interested in the librarian that he'd been receiving reports about him.

As far as she knew, Uncle Patch had never even stepped into the library before.

15

It had been a near escape. Another minute, and the queen would have kicked him out of the palace there and then. Fortunately Charleren had been a good sport about their fight. Alex would have tried to make the prince look better, to draw it out a bit more, but he didn't have *time*. Two days, and that was it. Really only a day and a half, now, to deal with something that was a much bigger problem than anyone else realized.

And when he got back to the library, he found that his pages had delivered a letter.

It was from one of the assistants to the librarian in Far Wrothing—the librarian who had written asking about the marked book she'd found.

To the Royal Librarian,
I regret to inform you . . .

Oh, *no.* Alex fell into the nearest chair. Had his warning gotten there too late? With his elbows on the reading table and his hands gripping his hair, he read the rest of the letter.

I regret to inform you that Librarian Hockett has most unexpectedly died. There was nothing suspicious about her death; she simply fell asleep at her desk while reading.

"Gah! You idiot," Alex mumbled. She hadn't fallen asleep, he felt sure of it. She'd been reading, yes, but the marked book had been set in her library like a trap.

He'd never met Librarian Hockett, but her death hit him hard. He'd tried to warn her. Maybe his letter *had* arrived too late. Frowning, he read on.

In your most alarming letter you asked about L.B.
Surely, Royal Librarian, you know more than any of us about the L.B.s, and you know exactly what happened sixty years ago.

Alex gritted his teeth. "If I *knew*," he growled at the letter, "would I be asking?"

At any rate, the less said about these things, the better.
I will be assuming Librarian Hockett's duties here.
Sincerely,
Maren Rumsey

And she hadn't sent the marked book as he had asked. The book that had, he felt absolutely certain, killed Hockett. How many more would die if he didn't stop this?

Idiot. He crumpled up the letter and hurled it across the room. One of his pages swooped down, picked it up, and dropped it in a garbage can.

He remembered what Librarian Hockett had written in her letter to him.

I rather fear that the presence of this marked book means that one of the L.B.s is hidden here in my library, though I have not yet been able to find it.

Blast it. Another librarian secret that he might never figure out.

One thing he felt certain of—there was an L.B. in the royal library. It was marking books with its symbol, setting those books like traps for anyone who read them.

Wait. She had said it was *hidden*. Lord Patch had pretty much admitted that he was searching for something hidden in the royal library. Was it one of the

L.B.s? And if it was, what did he want with it, especially if it was as dangerous as Alex suspected?

Well, Lord Patch wasn't going to tell him what he was up to. All Alex could do was try to find every one of the marked books before his time was up.

He didn't bother with sleep.

He spent the night hours clearing the room he judged to be the most secure. It was down a passage off the fourth-story balcony, a place he guessed was at about the center of the library. The room was hacked out of the cliff itself, four rock walls with bookshelves bolted into the stone, and a door made of heavy wood banded with iron and closed with a bolt and two padlocks that had only one key, which Alex kept in his pocket.

As he continued searching the library, he found five more books with the symbol burned into their covers. Because he knew how dangerous they were, he managed to keep from reading them—though it was definitely risky, for they almost caught him more than once. Wearing heavy leather gloves, and carrying each book with a pair of tongs that his pages had found for him, Alex brought them to the fortified room, chained each book to a shelf, and locked the door behind him.

Wearily he climbed the spiral staircase to the fifth level. All of the books he passed were still. Sleeping, maybe. It was the middle of the night. The air was icy cold.

And then he heard a thumping sound coming up the winding staircase; something banged against a railing, and then against a door frame, and came rattling along a row of books, which rustled and bumped in protest.

As he turned, his pages ghosted up, dropped something long and narrow at his feet, and faded away. Another page came closer with a light-well.

Alex bent and picked up the present. A leather belt and scabbard. And in it, a sword. Drawing the sword, he held it at arm's length. It was a narrow, keen-edged blade made of tempered steel by the finest weapon-smiths in faraway Reese. It fit his hand and was perfectly balanced. The pages had seen him fight yesterday. They knew he could use it. That they had given it to him meant they thought he would need it.

They were right. "Thanks," he said to them, and strapped the sword around his waist. Time to track down another marked book.

Taking the light-well from the page, Alex made his way down a passage, around a corner, to what seemed like a dead end. To either side were shelves of thick encyclopedias. In front of him was a blank rock wall.

One of his pages drifted up to his shoulder and hung there, waiting for his orders.

"Where?" he asked. His voice sounded muffled in the thick silence.

The page edged closer to the bookcase on Alex's left. He held up the light-well, and saw a single letter appear in ink on the white surface of the page.

P

He nodded, understanding. Taking a deep breath, he reached out to the encyclopedia that was marked on the spine with the letter *P*. With chilled fingers, he pulled it, leverlike, away from the shelf. As the thick book leaned toward him, the entire wall of books opened inward—it was a secret door.

Stale, dry air gusted out of the hidden room. Alex stepped into it, holding up the light-well. It flickered, barely penetrating shadows that seemed dense, solid . . . waiting. His feet scuffed through dust. In the silence, he heard the sound of his own heartbeat, a steady thumping that he could almost feel in his bones.

Thump-thump, thump-thump, thump-thump.

His breath came faster. The marked book had to be in here somewhere. Carefully he held up the flickering light-well to see the books on the shelves of the hidden room. He brushed away dust and cobwebs to read the titles on the spines of each one.

OSTEOGRAPHIA:
ANATOMY OF THE BONES

SUCCINCT DESCRIPTIONS
OF THE MUSCLES AND BONES
OF THE HUMAN BODY

TREATISE ON PHYSIOGNOMY

These were books on anatomy. The human body.
Bones and muscles and nerves . . .

And hearts.

Thump-thump, thump-thump, thump-thump.

It wasn't . . . his . . . heartbeat.

A rustling sound came from the shelf behind him.
Whirling, he held up the light-well. In its faint glow, he
saw a book face-out on the shelf. Its title was printed in
gold. *The Human Heart.* Below that, scorched into the
bloodred leather of the cover, was the mark.

It pulsed in the heartbeat rhythm. Then the beat
of it slowed.

Alex felt his own heartbeat slowing to match it.

Slower. His breath came short and black spots floated in front of his eyes. The book—it was trying to stop his heart—to kill him.

He tried raising his arms, but they were too heavy. The light-well fell out of his hand, bounced once on the floor, and rolled into a corner. Shadows advanced, pulsing with the heartbeat of the marked book. They closed in around him.

Alex clenched his teeth. "I . . . am . . . a *librarian*," he said. He forced himself to take a deep breath. Dying in battle was one thing, but his pa would be furious if he let himself be killed by a *book*.

A second later, the book shot off the shelf, aimed at Alex's head. He flung himself to the floor, and it slammed into the wall behind him.

"Nice try," he gasped, getting back to his feet, and with a ruffle of its pages, the book whirled and came back at him. Alex ducked, but not fast enough—the book bashed him in the arm, knocking him back into the shelves. Steadying himself, Alex snatched his sword from the scabbard. The blade gleamed in the light. With a shrieking-ripping sound, a page tore itself from the heart book and came at him, flashing through the air like a knife. He parried it, and then another, and the book came at him again, open this time. He caught a glimpse of an engraving of a heart with words written in bloodred ink writhing all around it. Knocking aside another arrowlike page, he lunged at the book, but it darted back, out of reach. The heart engraving pulsed, and he felt his own heart being squeezed. He gasped for breath. The heart's beating pounded in his ears. Darkness closed in around him. He heard a tearing sound, and another one of the book's pages arrowed toward him, and this time he was too slow, and felt a line of pain open along his cheek, just below his eye.

Then the book shot toward him.

With the very last of his strength, Alex raised the sword and flung it. Like a spear, it skewered the book, pinning it to the shelf behind it. The engraved heart, pierced through by the sharp point of the sword, gave one last echoing beat and went still. Bloody ink oozed from it, staining the page red and dripping onto the floor.

"I," Alex told it fiercely, "am a librarian."

In one stride he bounded across the room and jerked the sword out of the book. Before it could do anything else, he wiped the red ink off the end of the sword and sheathed it, pulled the woolly hat off his head, and shoved the book into it. It heaved and struggled as he wrapped his arms around it and hurried from the room. "Page!" he shouted as he stumbled into the darkened passageway. Seven worried pages appeared before him, one holding a light-well. "Close the door behind me," he ordered, and several of the pages fluttered to obey. Two more appeared carrying lights, leading him down the spiral staircase to the passage that led to the fortified room.

Shoving the struggling book under one arm, he pulled the key out of his pocket and opened the padlocks. As the door swung open, the other marked books chained to the shelves rattled and thumped.

"Stop it," Alex muttered. He went to one of the shelves that was bolted to the rock wall. He had a place ready. He pulled the book out of his hat and thrust it into a book-sized metal box. Slamming down the iron cover, he locked it, wrapped a chain around it, then secured it with the chain to the shelf.

He backed out of the room, locked it up again, and leaned against the wall, feeling weak at the knees. That had been close. Too close.

With chilled fingers he checked the cut on his face, blotting up the blood with his coat sleeve. Cheekbone. He was lucky it hadn't been his eye—he needed to be able to see to read. Wearily he straightened and started down the winding stairs.

Reaching the main floor, he realized that morning light was filtering through the grime-encrusted windows. He needed breakfast, and then to do his training—*with* a sword this time—and then he'd start hunting for the next marked book. He felt gritty, dusty, and fairly certain that the next one was going to be even more dangerous. He had to be ready for anything. "Page," he croaked, and four pages clustered around him. "Tea," he ordered, and trudged into his office, where he sat at his desk.

As he reached to pick up a book to read while he waited, the sleeve of his coat pulled back, and he saw the bracelet of words that encircled his wrist. With chilly fingertips he rubbed the letters. They were still as dark against his skin as they had been the day the mysterious Red Codex in his father's library had marked him.

Wait.

Marked him?

He remembered something he'd said to the queen when he'd been arguing with her. *I didn't choose to be a librarian . . . a librarian is what I am.*

Had the Red Codex marked him because it was choosing him? Had it made him a librarian? He still couldn't remember what the Codex had been about; he only knew that it'd had a red leather cover, and that he'd been completely absorbed in it, until the words had crawled out, over his hand, and around his wrist.

It had not been one of the marked books—there had been no symbol burned into its cover. At least, not that he remembered. It had attacked Jeffen and Franciss, so it had been dangerous. Possibly, as his former master, Merwyn Farnsworth, had said, it had been *the* codex. Whatever that meant.

Did the Red Codex that had marked him have anything to do with what was going on in the royal library?

Oh, blast. It must have. He just didn't know what. He pulled the coat sleeve down to cover the letters. With a sigh, he rubbed his eyes. There was way too much that he didn't know.

Then he heard the outer door of the library open and slam. He came out into the main room to see Charleren—good, right on time, Alex thought—but then he realized that the prince wasn't alone. His sister was with him.

Queen Kenneret stood in the watery gray light that trickled in through the high windows, gazing around the room. She wore a different kind of clothes, he realized. A dress that looked more simple, more comfortable, more warm. It didn't make her look any less queenly.

Seeing the library through her eyes, Alex felt himself cringe a little. Both of the long reading tables were covered with stacks of books, papers, dirty teacups, nubs of pencils, lengths of heavy chain and rusty padlocks, bottles of ink half used up, and the various presents that his pages kept bringing him, things like a tiny box of headache pills, a jeweled ring that he'd been meaning to return to the queen, and a selection of knitted woolly items like mittens and more hats and scarves. He'd shifted some of the clutter onto the floor to make room for his map, which took up half of one table. The map wasn't just one paper, but lots of them clipped together as he added to it, because the library was bigger and more sprawling than he'd realized.

The tables weren't even the worst of it. The cards from the catalog were strewn everywhere. Books were piled everywhere else. Half of the shelves were empty—the books kept sneaking off and hiding.

The queen put her hands on her hips. She did *not* look happy. Charleren stood beside her, his face blank. His nose was swollen up like a strawberry from their fight the day before.

"My uncle was right," the queen said sharply. "This is a disaster."

Alex felt all of his frustration, and weariness, and his annoyance that the library was *still* unheated, and the knowledge that Lord Patch seemed to have free access to it, and the fact that another librarian was dead and he had no idea what the L.B.s were, and his constant, nagging awareness that the books were afraid and he couldn't do much to protect them, and, yes, the fright of his close encounter with *The Human Heart* book—all of it hit him at the same time, so when he answered her, he wasn't at his most polite.

"What do you even know about it?" he snarled, and flung himself into a chair at the table.

"As much as you do, apparently," Kenneret answered. Her tone was frosty.

Alex gave her a sour look. "I *am* a librarian," he said. "For one more day, anyway."

"No," she said sharply. "You are not. You never were."

Alex sat up as shock flashed through him. "You're dismissing me?"

"Yes," she said.

"Then you're an idiot," he said bitterly, getting to his feet again so he could pace. "Your Majesty," he added, making the words drip with acid. "This"—he waved his arm, meaning the whole library—"is a disaster."

"That is what we just said." The queen was a lot shorter than he was, but somehow she managed to look down her nose at him, all snooty. "And you are out of line."

Her brother snorted, as if to say *So out of line.* And Alex knew it, he knew he was being disrespectful, but couldn't she see that the library was too *important* for politeness?

"We," the queen went on, "have seen a letter from Duchess Purslane."

Oh, *blast*. Alex sat down again with a thump.

"Can you guess what it says?" Kenneret asked, her voice edged.

Alex folded his arms on the table and rested his head on them. "Yes," he answered, his voice muffled. It was too much, after the night he'd had. He lifted his head again and rubbed his eyes. "The duchess said . . ." He considered it. "She said that Merwyn Farnsworth had an apprentice . . . no, a servant, probably, who is no librarian and who tried to destroy the papers in her library." He glanced up at her. She was frowning. "That's about the sum of it, I'm guessing."

"Not quite," she said. She held up the letter—he hadn't noticed that she was carrying it. Unfolding it, she read.

. . . the boy is a liar and a forger of letters.

She glanced at him.

Alex shrugged. It was essentially true.

He wanted to destroy my library.

Only sort of true, but explaining it wasn't going to help.

After a moment, the queen went on.

The boy was after Merwyn Farnsworth's job. I would not be at all surprised to discover that he was responsible for the librarian's death, perhaps even intentionally caused it.

"What?" Alex shook his head. "No! That part of it is wrong."

"Only that part?"

"Yes," he admitted. "But you already knew that."

"Charlie, throw him out."

Alex gave him a look that said *Just try*. "No," he said, and as Kenneret turned to leave he jumped to his feet and grabbed her arm.

"Careful," Charlie said warningly.

"Listen," Alex said, getting desperate. "You can't— I know it looks bad, but I do know what I'm doing." Mostly. "What if I can prove that there are dangerous books here in the library?"

Kenneret straightened and looked down at his hand, which was still on her arm. Quickly he snatched it away. Then she looked him over, from head to toe, and even though he was a good five inches taller than she was, she made him feel small and grubby. She was *such* a queen. "How do you do it?" she asked musingly.

"Do what?" he said.

"I never gave the library a single thought before you came. Somehow you make it seem like the most important thing in the world."

"Because it *is*—" he started.

"I'm missing a meeting right now with the trade minister. My uncle will be so disappointed in me. Why am I even here?" she asked herself. With a shake of her head, as if she was waking herself up, she turned away and started for the door.

For a second, Alex felt like his feet were too heavy to move, because he knew this was it, he was done here. Then he went after her. "Wait." As she reached the door, he slid in front of her, blocking her way. "Kenneret, just listen," he said hurriedly. "This is important, hugely important, and it does want your attention. The library's been neglected for far too long, and if you let it go any farther, there will be trouble."

She stood there looking up at him, with her brother looming at her back.

With a cold feeling in his stomach, he realized that he'd just called her by her first name, instead of *Your Majesty.*

A line of a frown gathered between her eyebrows. "What happened to your face?" she asked after a long moment.

"A book," he answered.

"It gave you a paper cut?" Charleren put in.

"No," Alex said, giving him a glare that said *Stay out of it.* Then he changed his tone. "Actually, yes. It attacked me." He turned his attention back to the queen. "And I can prove it. Will you come and see?"

For a moment she wavered. Then she glanced over his head. He didn't know what she saw, but it made her give a decisive nod. "All right, Alex. Show me. But if this is a lie, you really will be dismissed. The guards will throw you out of here so fast, your head will spin."

"Why is it so cold in here?" Kenneret asked, as Alex led her and Charlie across the cluttered main room of the library.

"You tell me," she thought she heard Alex mutter.

He stalked ahead of them, his hands thrust into his coat pockets, looking typically annoyed, but not very typically weary, as if he hadn't slept in days. He was wearing a sheathed sword. He couldn't see them, but a swarm of pages followed him, hovering almost protectively right behind his back. She knew about librarians' pages, of course, but she'd always thought they had one or two, not twenty or thirty, as Alex had. With that many pages at his service, he *had* to be a librarian, despite what Uncle Patch had said about him. Didn't he? She wanted to believe that he was.

The first thing that morning, while she'd been eating toast and tea for breakfast, her uncle had joined her.

"Kenneret," he said, his voice serious, pulling up a chair at the table, "I have received most disturbing news." And then he'd given her the letter from Duchess Purslane. As Kenneret scanned the letter, she felt a cold heaviness in her chest. She had met the duchess before; the woman was obsessed with roses and her family history, she recalled, and was solid and law-abiding, one of the old nobility. She wouldn't invent the terrible things she had written about Alex. So they had to be true.

She didn't want them to be true. She'd read through the letter again, and set it on the table. Carefully she picked up her cup and took a sip of tea. Then she set it down and took a neat bite of toast.

"So you see, my dear," her uncle had said, "the boy is not a librarian at all, but a thief, a liar, and possibly a murderer. Really, he ought to be imprisoned and sent back to Purslane to face punishment for his crimes. I don't want to worry you with this. I will see to it that guards are sent to the library to arrest him."

For just a moment, Kenneret had felt relief. Yes.

Uncle Patch could take care of it. She didn't need to worry. The library wasn't that important anyway. She took another bite of toast. Then she scolded herself. She was queen. It shouldn't be easy; she *did* need to worry.

"I will see to dismissing the royal librarian," she'd said to her uncle.

For just a fraction of a second, the briefest loss of control, an expression flashed across his face. Almost a snarl.

And then he was all bland smiles again. "Of course, Kennie. You do what you feel you must."

She had brought a set of four guards with her. They were waiting outside the library door. All she had to do was call them.

"Up here," Alex said, starting up a spiral staircase that led them past the first two levels of books to the third level. "Light-wells," he muttered, and two of his pages swooped away, then reappeared a moment later carrying lights, which they held, floating ahead of them down a narrow corridor lined with bookshelves. *Stolen* light-wells, Kenneret reminded herself.

They reached a door, one that looked heavy and solid.

Alex reached into his coat pocket. In the wavery light, she saw him go pale, paler than he already was.

"Blast it," she heard him whisper.

"What?" she whispered back.

"Key's already in the lock," he said in a normal voice, and pointed, and she saw that yes, one of the padlocks that secured the door had a key in it.

"So you left it there?" she asked, not sure what was going on.

"No." He shook his head. "I put it in my pocket." He turned his intense stare on her. "I'm very careful with the key to this particular room. It shouldn't be here." He turned to the door again. "But it is. They want to escape."

"The books do?" Charlie put in from behind her. Alex shot him a scornful look, and Charlie squirmed a bit. "I was only asking," he protested.

Opening both padlocks, Alex pushed open the heavy door. The two pages holding light-wells floated into the room before them. It was made all of stone, with a low ceiling and just a few shelves.

"See?" Alex said, pointing. "Dangerous."

Five books were there, wrapped in chains or stuffed into locked metal boxes, all chained to the shelves. "I see," Kenneret said slowly, "that you have secured all of these books."

"They're not *doing* anything," Charlie said.

Alex glared at the books. "No," he muttered after a few silent moments had passed. "They're not."

They sat there, like every book Kenneret had ever seen, gathering dust. She was starting to wonder if maybe Alex was crazy. Did he think the books moved around? Did he really believe a book—a *book*!—had attacked him and given him the nasty cut on his face? Or that the books had somehow stolen the key to this room and were actively trying to escape? It *was* crazy! And if he was that crazy, maybe he really *had* killed old Merwyn Farnsworth.

And here she was, the queen, in a small room with him, with only her brother, who Alex, she suspected, could probably take apart with his little finger. And he was wearing a sword. The guards were outside the library's main door, but it would take them too long to get up here even if they could hear her shout for them.

She felt a frisson of fear creep up the back of her neck.

"This . . ." Alex said, his voice wavering. "This isn't the . . ." He shook his head. "This isn't the thing I was going to show you," he said briskly, and picked up a length of chain from one of the shelves. "I was just getting this." He spun and strode past her, out of the room.

"It's all right, Kennie," her brother whispered as they turned to follow him. "He really is a librarian."

She was becoming more certain that he was *not*. Still, she watched Alex carefully lock the door behind them and then let him lead them up another level and down a winding passageway.

Two paces ahead, Alex said something to one of his pages, and it whirled off, followed by three others. He led them around two more corners, up a short flight of stone stairs, around another corner—she'd had *no* idea the library was this extensive—to a big circular room with a ceiling that was made entirely of glass. A reading room. The ceiling-window was dirty and scattered with leaves, but it let in enough light to show a room that had been abandoned for a long time. Dust lay thick on the floor, unmarked by footsteps. Dusty cobwebs draped the books on the shelves.

Alex paused in the arched doorway and cocked his head, as if listening for something.

All was still. She heard nothing.

"Wait here," he ordered, and then stepped into the room. Puffs of dust rose up at every footstep, and then settled again. When he reached the center of the room, he paused. And waited.

Kenneret stood there in the doorway, with Charlie's warm bulk beside her. She felt wound tight, even a little frightened, expecting something to happen, and then chided herself. Nothing was going to happen. Alex, she thought sadly, really was crazy and had done all the terrible things the letter had said he'd done.

And for long minutes, nothing did happen.

She was just opening her mouth to call an end to it when Alex raised his hand. He'd gone on alert, poised, listening.

"It's here," he said softly.

The sound of his voice was answered by a faint rustling sound, like pages turning.

But nothing in the room had moved.

Then, the faintest of breezes brushed through the dust at the edges of the room. Kenneret shivered. How had it gotten so cold? Icy cold. Another tendril of air snaked across the room, sending up a swirl of dust that spiraled and then settled to the floor.

That was enough. Alex went into action. "This is a room full of books about the weather," he said quickly. Two of his pages swooped in, carrying a metal box. "One of the books is marked with a symbol," Alex said as the box dropped onto the floor at his feet with a thump and a billow of dust. "It will come for us," he went on. "Be ready for anything. It's going to be bad."

As he spoke, the breeze picked up; dust swirled in

little eddies around the room. The glass in the ceiling-window rattled.

"Stay there, Kenneret," he ordered. "Charlie, I'm going to need your help."

With a whoop of excitement, her brother bounded into the room.

At the same moment, there was a rumble from the shelf behind Alex. All at once, the tendrils of air turned into a torrent of wind that shrieked around the room. It ripped books off the shelves and sent them whirling, pages flapping. Sudden rain pelted down, followed by an icy blast of snow.

"Look out!" she heard Alex shout. A bolt of lightning crashed across the room.

Kenneret braced herself against the doorway, buffeted by wind, slashed with curtains of rain. Looking up, she saw that a roiling, greenish-black cloud had gathered just below the glass ceiling. It rumbled with thunder. She heard her brother shout. Books hurtled through the air, and she saw Alex and Charlie duck. A book glanced off Alex's arm and then one slammed into his back, and he stumbled.

Another bolt of lightning crackled across the room, bouncing from one wall to the next. Then it slowed, turned, and seemed to fix on Alex in the center of the room.

"Duck!" Charlie shouted.

Alex flung himself to the floor, and the bolt flashed over his head, slamming into the shelf of books behind him with an explosion of sparks. The wind whooshed past, and as Alex climbed to his feet, a book came flying at him; he blocked it with his arm, and then another one came. A roar of rain exploded in front of him, and then four more books spun toward his head.

Without hesitating, he drew his sword and blocked the books as they came at him, knocking them to the floor.

Then another book floated closer to him. It hung in a bubble of stillness in the midst of the wildly blowing wind, the rain, the snow. Slowly the book opened. Its pages fluttered, almost as if they were beckoning. She saw Alex lower the sword and take a step closer to it, fascinated, and then he threw his arm over his eyes. "Charlie!" he shouted, his voice hoarse, and her brother was at his shoulder. "Get it!"

The book retreated, and Charlie dove after it, grabbing it and slamming it shut. As he popped the bubble around it, the wind howled, thunder roared, and the ceiling shattered, raining shards of glass all around them. Charlie had the book in his arms, wrestling it to the floor.

"Hold on," Alex ordered, and dropping the sword,

he snatched up the iron box from where it sat on the floor. "Don't let it open. Get it in." He grabbed one end of the book, and he and Charlie wrestled with it, trying to get it into the box.

"Kennie, we need you!" Charlie shouted.

Releasing her grip on the door frame, Kenneret hurried to help. As she entered the room, the rain pounded down on her head. She pushed dripping tendrils of hair out of her eyes and went to kneel beside the boys. Charlie and Alex were holding on to the book, which struggled wildly in their hands. Its cover, she saw, was coated with ice—in a moment it would slither away from them. And she saw, in the center of the cover, a pulsing, burned-black symbol outlined in ember-bright orange. It was the same symbol that Alex had drawn in the dirt when he'd talked to her in the garden.

But this version seemed alive, poisonous, deadly.

"Hurry!" gasped Alex, and pointed with his chin at the box.

It was made of iron and had a hinged lid. With cold fingers, she opened it, then pushed it closer.

Alex met her eye. "Ready?"

She gave him a brisk nod.

With a shout, he and Charlie heaved the book into the box.

"Close it, close it!" Charlie panted, and he barely got his fingers out of the way as she slammed the box shut. Abruptly, the wind stopped. A few last drops of rain pattered down around them. Overhead, the thick cloud dissipated, and sunlight peeked in through the shattered ceiling-window. Glinting shards of glass were scattered all over the floor, along with soaking wet books and torn-out pages. One wall of books was scorched from the blast of lightning that had hit it.

Alex was already wrapping a length of heavy chain around the box. Without even looking up, he took the padlock that one of his pages was holding at his shoulder, and then he locked the chain. From inside the box came the sound of bumping and thumping. The book was trying to get out.

"Phew!" Charlie said, sitting back and wiping wet hair out of his face. He had watery blood streaming from a cut on the back of his hand. "Who knew books could be so exciting?"

"I did," Alex said. And then, to Kenneret's astonishment, he grinned at her. Climbing wearily to his feet, he bent to offer her his hand.

She took it, and let him pull her up, then looked him over. His eyes almost glowed with excitement, as the last of the rain dripped off the end of his nose. The wind had left his hair looking like a tumbled haystack. He really did seem crazed. He did *not* look like a librarian.

Charlie had gotten to his feet and stood watching them, his arms folded, his face blank. She had always assumed that the blank face meant that his mind was empty, too, but after this morning she wasn't so certain. "How did you know that Alex was a librarian?" she asked him.

Charlie shrugged his broad shoulders. "The candles," he said. When she raised her eyebrows, he went on. "When I first came to the library, I brought candles in with me. He didn't like it. I figured he didn't want the books burning up."

It had taken her longer than that to realize about the candles. Her brother was a lot smarter than he let on, Kenneret guessed.

"And," Charlie added, "because he can fight like that—like he did yesterday—but he doesn't call himself a sword fighter. He calls himself a librarian. So he must be one, right?"

Kenneret nodded. She knew that to Charlie, that made sense.

She was sure she looked as bedraggled as Alex did. The crown had stayed on her head only because it was pinned to her sodden braids, and her dress was wet through. But she gathered her queenliness around her, straightened, and spoke clearly. "You are not Merwyn Farnsworth."

"No," Alex answered, meeting her gaze.

"You were his apprentice?" she asked.

"Sort of." He shrugged. "He barely taught me anything." And then he added quickly, "And I did not kill him."

"Did you try to destroy Duchess Purslane's books?" she went on.

"Useless papers," he said. "And old diaries. Not books."

"We suppose that you had a good reason."

"I did." He had started to shiver. The room was cold enough that the puddles of rain already had a slick of ice on them.

Her toes felt frozen, even inside her fur-lined boots. She needed to settle this. "Well then," she said. Her uncle was going to be unhappy with her. But it would be good for Charlie, she thought, and, well, before all of this had started, she'd had a certain idea of a librarian in her head: a cranky old lady or ancient, beardy man with thick spectacles and an abstracted air, almost as dusty as the books she or he put in order, and always bristling with keys that they used to keep their libraries locked up tight.

Librarians, it turned out, were nothing like that.

This librarian was cranky, true, but he was young, and he carried a sword, which he knew how to use. He'd told her before that books were dangerous, and now she believed him. She took a deep breath. "Alex," she said, using her most queenly voice. She realized that she needed to learn the rest of his name, and who he really was. But not now. "We ask you to remain here, and we name you, officially, the royal librarian."

She expected him to be grateful, at least. But he was Alex, so he wasn't ever going to act in an expected way.

"Good," he said, instead of *thank you.* "The first thing we need is heat for the library." Then he gave her another one of his surprising grins. "That's the librarian *we,* in case you didn't know. I speak for myself, and for the books. It's freezing in here! The books don't like it, and neither do I." Without waiting for her to comment, he went on, looking around the reading room full of weather books. "I'll have to get these books dried out and see what can be salvaged. And I'm going to need another assistant. Or two. And—"

She held up a hand, and was surprised when he fell silent and raised his eyebrows, waiting to see what she wanted.

"So you accept the position?" she asked.

Beside her, Charlie burst out laughing. "Of course he does, Kennie!"

Alex studied them both, the level gaze that she was starting to get used to. "I *am* a librarian," he said with exasperating confidence. It made her want to bare her teeth at him and growl. "But yes, I accept the position." And then he added, just to twist the knife a bit, "Your Majesty."

17

Kenneret had been queen now for almost four months.

Being *Your Majesty* was still new.

So much about being queen was new.

Four months ago she had turned sixteen. Ordinarily, a regent like her uncle ran the kingdom until the young prince or princess was eighteen, the right age for taking over.

Kenneret had assumed that Uncle Patch would do the same, but suddenly something had changed. *He* had changed. Without any warning, he had announced that she would be crowned on her birthday.

"I don't feel ready," she had told him. She'd thought

she'd have years more to prepare.

"My dear," he had said smoothly, "you are exceptionally mature and intelligent, a born leader. What better time than now for you to become queen?"

And so, despite her secret doubts, she had agreed.

She'd had no *idea* what it meant to be queen. It wasn't glamorous or glittering, it was brute hard work and long hours. And it was, quite often, lonely. The crown she wore was gold, but it was heavy—and it made her head ache.

Kenneret had barely gotten dried off and warmed up after the encounter with the marked weather book in the library, when she was back in her office studying a sheaf of papers about the Greylings on the northern border.

The Greylings were not one single nation, but a bunch of clans, each with a different leader, and very difficult to keep track of. You couldn't negotiate a peace with one of the clan leaders, because the clan would simply replace him or her and declare the treaty null and void, and start raiding across the border again. They were infuriating, persistent, and most of them were brilliant fighters. Not a comfortable northern neighbor *at all*.

Something in the papers she was studying didn't make sense. Wanting an explanation, she went in search of the foreign minister to see what he could tell her. Steward Dorriss went with her.

She found the minister in her uncle's office.

"Uncle," she said coolly as she entered the gold-and-black room. She nodded at the minister, who had stood up from a brocade chair and was bowing.

Her uncle looked faintly annoyed. Which meant that he was extremely upset. Her eye for detail showed that he was on edge. Not his usual bland self.

Three months ago, seeing this, she might have retreated, and apologized, and tried to be *nice*.

Now she could feel her steward behind her, radiating disapproval. Kenneret knew what Dorriss would say.

She didn't need the reminder. To be queen. Instead of stuttering out an explanation of why she had come, she simply stood there and raised her eyebrows, waiting.

The minister broke first, of course. "Your Majesty," he said quickly. "Lord Patch and I were, ah, discussing the Greyling situation."

"We are aware," she said calmly. "Do you not think the queen should have been invited to join you?"

Her uncle had gotten to his feet. He had *not* bowed, Kenneret realized. He never bowed. She'd never thought he should, before.

Now she wasn't so sure.

"The Greyling situation is hopelessly tangled," Uncle Patch said. He came around from behind his desk. "You have enough to deal with, my dear, without worrying about that rat's nest." He took her by the elbow, as if he was going to steer her toward the door.

Instead of moving, she glanced aside at him, meeting his eyes. She studied him carefully. His blank, bland mask was firmly in place. She could not see that there was anything wrong.

But she had the strongest feeling that there *was* something wrong. She just didn't know what.

So she decided to test him, just a bit.

She turned to the minister, who was watching them with wide eyes. "We are certain," she said to him, "that Lord Patch has been telling you that the Greylings are not a threat to the kingdom."

"Indeed, no," the minister blurted out. "I assumed that Your Majesty had ordered—"

"Yes, yes," her uncle interrupted, allowing a tinge of impatience to creep into his voice. "We do not need to speak further about it now." His pressure on her elbow increased. He *really* wanted her to leave.

She refused to budge. "Tell us more," she said to the minister.

His eyes darted between her and her uncle. "His

Lordship has been saying that we must use our military might to crush the Greylings, and push the border outward."

"Has he?" Kenneret prompted.

"Yes!" the minister said eagerly. "He said that Aethel could be so much greater than a country full of dirt-grubbing farmers, if only we can expand our borders." He gave a nervous smile. "Your uncle has vision, Your Majesty. We were just drawing up plans to add an army to the Swift's forces in the north."

"We see," Kenneret said, feeling almost sad. Her uncle did not trust her to make important decisions. Maybe he was trying to protect her.

Instead of sighing about that, she lifted her chin. "We will not be summoning an army, nor will we be inciting war with our northern neighbors. And henceforth," she said to the minister, who looked pale and clammy, "you will make certain that all information about the Greylings is shared with the queen."

"Y-yes, Your Majesty," the minister mumbled. "Of course." He bowed, and then bowed again.

"I will see to it, Your Majesty," Dorriss put in.

"Good." Kenneret looked down at her uncle's hand, still on her elbow. His fingers were digging into her arm. She looked up and saw that his face was rigid—with fury. A second ticked by, and then another, and his grip on her arm relaxed.

"Very well done, my dear," he said softly, so only she could hear. "You are far better at this than I expected you would be."

She didn't know what answer to give, so she nodded and turned to leave the room, her skirts swirling around her ankles.

She didn't rub the place on her arm where he'd been holding her. But she'd find bruises there later, she felt sure.

18

Hearing the library door slam, Alex came out of his office. He'd spent the whole previous day trying to save the books from the weather room. Half of them had been scorched by lightning and might not be salvageable. The other half had been drenched, so he'd strung up clotheslines in his office and hung the books there to dry. It had taken most of the night, and he seriously did not have time for this kind of task, not with the marked books on the loose. Now he was groggy after not enough sleep. His hands were wrapped around a cup of tea that his pages had brought him.

Prince Charleren, he saw, had brought practice

swords to his first day of work when he would actually be working.

"Royal librarian," Alex growled, pointing to himself. "*Not* a sword teacher."

"So cranky in the mornings," Charlie said cheerfully, and dumped the swords on the nearest reading table. "The lighter one's for you, since you're not as muscley as I am." He pulled something else wrapped in a napkin out of the pocket of his fine velvet coat and handed it to Alex. "And I brought this as a bribe."

Alex sniffed the package. It smelled delicious, like cinnamon and sugar. Unwrapping the napkin, he found a spiced butter-bun, still warm from the oven. A few seconds later he'd devoured it, down to the last crumb. Feeling a little better, he went to the table, where he set down his teacup. He'd eaten the bribe, and he needed to do his training anyway.

"All right," he said, picking up a practice sword. "Let's see how long it will take you to die in a fight." He took a big, obvious swing at Charlie's head.

The other boy ducked. "Hey, I wasn't ready," he protested.

Alex gave him an edged smile. "Oh dear me. I'm so terribly sorry, Your Royal Uselessness."

With a roar, Charlie grabbed his sword and came after Alex.

So they had a fine lesson on how fighting while angry was the best way to die quickly in a fight, or at the very least end up with a lot of bruises. This was a lesson that Alex had learned himself many, many times, so he was very happy to pass it along to Charlie.

"It's a good thing these are practice swords," Charlie said ruefully, when they'd finished. "Or it'd be awfully bloody in here. All my blood, of course." Pushing up his sleeve, he inspected a nasty bruise on his arm, then held it up to show it off.

"Nice one," Alex said.

Charlie grinned at him.

And Alex found himself, suddenly and unexpectedly, liking the prince enormously. As if the other boy was, of all things, a *friend*. Still holding the practice sword, he studied Charlie.

Who turned a little red under Alex's scrutiny. "What?" he asked.

"I can't imagine not being able to read," Alex said bluntly. He wasn't used to admitting how he really felt about things, but he added, "Books—reading—it's more important to me than anything."

"Even training with the sword?" Charlie asked, rolling down his sleeve again and buttoning the cuff.

"I do that because I have to." Alex balanced the

practice sword on the palm of his hand. "Not because I love it."

"But you're *good*," Charlie protested.

Alex shrugged. "It's just because I've trained from the time I could walk. Anybody would be good with that kind of work. But find somebody who actually loves the sword, and give him or her that kind of training, and they'd destroy me. Easy."

Charlie's face had gone blank, as if his eyes were looking inward. "I do," he said quietly. "I love it that much. Not being able to read—it's not so bad, really. I'd give anything to have the training that you did." And with about as much subtlety as a boulder, he added, "Uh, by the way, who taught you the sword?"

Friend or not, that was *not* something Alex wanted to talk about. "None of your business." He tossed the sword onto the table; it landed with a clatter. "Bring one of those buns again tomorrow," he said, and headed back into his office to fetch his coat.

When he'd washed and dressed, he got to work.

The map of the royal library had gotten big enough that he'd had to lay it out on the floor, encircled by light-wells. Not stolen light-wells, incidentally, but ones that a footman had delivered to him. Queen's orders.

The library was warm, too. Well heated.

For about five minutes, Alex had felt relieved that the queen had officially appointed him the royal librarian. It meant he couldn't be tossed out of the palace, at least not without a fuss. It meant he and the books had light and heat. It would give him time to set things right.

Yet he felt more and more direly certain that they were running out of time. He had quarantined six books so far, and the one in the weather room had been the worst one yet. For every one he dealt with, he knew that more were being marked, but he didn't know what was marking them. And there were whole sections of the library that he hadn't found yet, either.

For now, he was in danger—he knew that much for sure. But if he didn't get this dealt with, and *soon*, the danger could spread. It made sense to him now why librarians were so obsessive about keeping books locked up.

He wondered if he should try to quarantine every single book in the palace. There must be books that had been taken out of the library, especially as the old royal librarian had been so incompetent.

No. He didn't have time. He'd just have to work as fast as he could to figure out what was happening.

Why the books were being marked—*what* was marking them. And what it meant for the library.

He knelt on the floor, examining the map.

Charlie was sitting at one of the reading tables, not reading, of course, or doing anything useful, but tipped back in his chair, tossing a balled-up mitten into the air and catching it, over and over. It was getting on Alex's nerves.

Trying to ignore Charlie, he focused on the map. He'd drawn an *X* on every place where he'd found one of the marked books. Was there a pattern to it? He couldn't tell. If there was, he might be able to predict where the next marked book would appear.

Hmmm, Alex thought. If there *was* a pattern, what would it mean? He got up and walked around to crouch on the other side of the map, studying it carefully.

A balled-up mitten bonked Alex in the head and fell onto the map. Startled, he glared at Charlie. "The books didn't like it, you said," Charlie said.

The prince's broad face looked suspiciously benign. "You told my sister that the books didn't like the cold. How do you know they didn't?"

Alex picked up the mitten and hurled it back at Charlie. Missed. Then he gave the prince his best *you are an idiot* stare, the one that had been known to make grown men and women armed with swords tremble in their boots.

The stare missed Charlie too, because he only grinned in response. "I know, I know," the prince said. "It's because you're a . . ." He lowered his voice, making it portentous. "A *librarian*." With a thump, he set all four legs of his chair on the floor again. "But *how* did you *know* they didn't like the cold?"

Well now. That was an interesting question. Alex got to his feet and went to fetch the mitten. Finding it behind the card catalog, he brought it back, dropping it onto the table beside Charlie. "How do I know," he repeated. Absently he rubbed the bracelet of words printed around his left wrist.

Charlie leaned over and handed him the mitten-ball. "You'll need the thinking-mitten for this."

"Thinking-mitten," Alex repeated dubiously as he tipped back in a chair. He tossed the mitten-ball up, caught it, then tossed it again. He sat looking up, five stories up, to the shadowed ceiling of the library's main room. The bird books were flapping around up there again. He wouldn't be surprised if they'd built nests atop the very highest shelves. "How do I know?" he muttered again.

Closing his eyes, he thought about the books. Shelf after shelf, room after room, the whole library, at least what he'd mapped so far. And he could *feel* it. The books were uneasy. They were frightened—it was like a tremble in the air, a slightly creepy feeling. It was something only a librarian could sense. Like an itch. The books were out of place. There was no order. And that wasn't all. He could feel the marked books, too, and something else that felt almost . . . rotten. It was all *wrong*.

This wasn't something he could explain to Charlie, of all people. Opening his eyes, Alex tossed the balled-up mitten back to him. "Because I'm a librarian," he said.

Charlie rolled his eyes.

Before Alex could explain further, three of his pages zipped out of a passageway on the fourth level and shot down like swooping hawks to place themselves in front of Alex's eyes.

"Yipes," Charlie said. "Scary when they do that."

Ignoring him, Alex grabbed the first page and read the message that was spilling out in ink across the white paper.

Found, the page wrote. *Found.*

"Found what?" Alex demanded.

The second page floated closer, edging the first page out of the way. *Bug,* it wrote.

Alex frowned. "You found a bug?"

"Is that a bad thing?" Charlie asked.

Gah. "Yes. Bugs are worse than bad." Alex jumped to his feet. "They eat paper, glue, bindings. Could be roaches. Or silverfish. Or biscuit beetles. Ugh, I hope it's not biscuit beetles." He grabbed the third page. "What kind of frass have you found?"

BUG! the page wrote.

"No help at all," Alex muttered, tossing the page behind him.

"What's frass?" Charlie asked.

"Bug droppings," Alex said briefly, crossing to the stairs. Charlie followed him up toward the fourth level. "Tells you what kind of bugs you've got." Then Alex stopped short, almost falling when Charlie bumped into him from behind. "Oh, *blast* it. Into a hundred thousand bug-infested pieces."

"What?" Charlie asked, righting himself.

"The cold." He turned to face the other boy. "If there are bugs in the books it's my own stupid fault." He clenched his fists. "One way to deal with insects in a library," he explained, "is to freeze the books. Kills the bugs. By asking your sister to heat the library, I practically invited the bugs in." He turned to hurry up the stairs again.

At the fourth level, the three pages led them along the curving balcony to a passageway that Alex hadn't had time yet to explore very carefully. The passage wound around and grew more and more narrow until they were edging sideways past shelves of books. Alex squeezed through until he came to the passage's end.

"Alex," Charlie said from behind him, his voice muffled. "I'm stuck."

"Just wait there," Alex told him, and took a light-well from one of his pages. Lifting it, he examined the dead end. The top of his head brushed the ceiling. Taking a book off a shelf at random, Alex checked it for traces of bug infestation. The paper was yellowed and crumbling, and smelled rather alarmingly damp, but there were no nibbled holes, no sign of insects, no frass.

A page carrying another light-well fluttered past his shoulder and down to Alex's knee level. The light glinted on metal. Crouching, Alex saw brass hinges. Carefully he wedged his fingers between the edge of the shelf and the wall, and pulled. With a hiss, a knee-high, square door slid out, and then aside. Alex peered in.

On the other side of the small door was a cave, a rather cozy round room carved from the rock. Its ceiling was lined with light-wells. It contained a nest of blankets and pillows, a few boxes, and hundreds of books.

Squatting like a cricket in the middle of the room, staring at him, was a person—a little, impossibly ancient, female person. She was dressed in layers of rags, and her feet were bare; she had a snarl of cobweb-white hair, and wore spectacles with lenses an inch thick. They made her eyes look huge in her small, wizened face.

"Let me guess," Alex said. Instead of crawling into the cave, he stayed in the low doorway. He didn't want to frighten her. "You're Bug."

He heard Charlie's voice from the passageway beyond. "Who're you talking to?"

At the sound, the old woman's magnified eyes blinked rapidly. Her bony hands gripped each other.

"Never mind him," Alex said to the old woman. "He's an idiot."

"I heard that," came Charlie's muffled voice.

Alex settled down to sit cross-legged in the low doorway, and examined the cave-room. It was stacked with books. "I see you're interested in gardening," he said to her. He tilted his head so he could see the titles of some of the other books. "And astronomy. And . . . huh. Love poetry."

The big bug-eyes widened.

"I'm a librarian," he told her.

The old lady's lips moved. "Librarian?" Her voice

was so faint, he almost couldn't hear it.

"Yep." Alex noted the two nearly transparent pages that floated behind her shoulder. They must have brought her supplies so that she didn't shrivel up and die in here. "And I'm guessing you're the old librarian's assistant. The steward told me you've been lost in here for years."

"No." Her eyes blinked rapidly. "Not lost," she whispered. "Hiding."

"Hiding from what?" Alex asked.

"*You* know." Her lips moved again. Alex waited, keeping a grip on his patience, until she went on. "It burns them with its mark."

"*What?*" he said sharply. "Its mark? The symbol?" He leaned closer. "Is it the L.B.?"

Bug's bony hands clutched each other. "The Lost Books, yes."

"*Lost Books,*" Alex breathed. So that was it.

"The bad books," she whispered. "The bad bad books."

"What *are* they?" Alex asked. "Besides *Lost* and *bad.* Be specific, if you can. I don't want to hear any vague, dire warnings."

"But if you are a librarian," Bug said, and her little wizened face crinkled into a frown, "how can you not know?"

Alex held on to his temper with both hands. "Tell me."

"All right," she whispered. "A proper librarian would know this already, but I will tell what I know, which isn't much because I am a lowly assistant." Her big eyes blinked accusingly at him. "*Not* a librarian." She made herself more comfortable, wrapping skinny arms around her legs and resting her chin on her knees. "Long ago—" she began.

"Sixty years ago?" Alex interrupted.

She gave him a long, buglike stare.

To his own surprise, Alex found himself apologizing. "Sorry, sorry. Go on. Tell what you know."

"Long ago," the old lady went on, "sixty years ago, the libraries were open. All the people read books. The people were curious. They looked out at the world, and traveled, and asked questions, and that made them want to read more books, and write them, too. Then some special books were written. The Lost Books. The people who wrote them had exceptional talents. A king, I think, and a warrior, and a whatsit, the one with the locks, and were there . . ." Her voice faded until Alex had to lean closer to hear her next words. "Three of them? Or were there four. Or five. Were there five?"

"Stay focused," Alex ordered.

Bug blinked her magnified eyes. "Yes. I don't know

how many. The Lost Books were written with magical ink, magical paper, magical pens, and when they were finished, the ... the ... the ..."

"The what?" Alex prompted.

"I don't know what to call it," Bug whispered. "The spirit, maybe. The self. The magic killed the body of each writer and drew the self of each writer into the books they were writing. They became trapped there."

"Wait," Alex interrupted. He rubbed his forehead, trying to get his brain to think it through. "You're basically saying that each of these books—the Lost Books—is alive?"

"All books are alive," Bug pointed out.

"I know that," Alex shot back.

"Good," Bug said primly. "Because that's something a librarian would know. But these books are different. Ordinary books do not *do*. Their purpose is to be read, that is all. The Lost Books *do*. They are powerful. Whoever reads them gets their power. It is why they were made."

"Alive and powerful," Alex repeated. "A king, you said, a warrior, a *whatsit with the locks*, and two more?" he asked.

Bug nodded. "Or three." She counted on her fingers, her lips moving.

"So one of these Lost Books must be hidden in the

royal library," Alex concluded. "And, what, it's woken up? Did the librarians put them to sleep, then?"

"It wasn't that easy," Bug put in. "They had to fight."

Alex studied her. "Did *you* fight?"

She curled more tightly into herself and nodded. "The librarians had to settle *all* the books, not just the Lost Books. They put *all* the books to sleep."

"Sixty years ago," Alex finished for her. "The librarians won their fight against the Lost Books and closed the libraries. They became guardians." He felt a deep satisfaction, finally knowing the answers to the questions that had been plaguing him ever since the Red Codex in his father's library had marked him. Was it a Lost Book? It hadn't had the symbol on it, and it hadn't been about Kings or Wars or Lockpicking . . .

The Red Codex was a mystery. Still, he wasn't going to show the mark it had made on his wrist to Bug, at least not now. It would frighten her, he was sure, just as it had frightened Merwyn Farnsworth.

"One of the Lost Books has woken up," he repeated, thinking it through. "No wonder the other books are so uneasy." Plus, he felt almost certain, Lord Patch was searching for the Lost Book, maybe making the library even *more* uneasy. He frowned and kept talking, thinking aloud. "Why is the Lost Book marking other books with a symbol? It's like . . . it's turning them into weapons. Why would it do that?"

Bug gazed at him, her eyes wide, magnified by her spectacles. "The Lost Book is dangerous. It turns the other books evil."

"Books are not evil," Alex said.

"Yes, they are. They came for my librarian. They will come for you, too." Bug was trembling so much that her voice shook. "Hide. You should hide. Don't let them find you."

Her fear felt almost contagious in the small space. The cave didn't seem cozy anymore, but confining. "Maybe you didn't hear me properly before," Alex said, getting to his feet. He crouched and peered back into the cave to fix Bug with his most inimical glare. "I'm a librarian. It's my job to deal with the Lost Books. And you, Miss Bug, are my new assistant."

She gulped, and her eyes grew even wider.

"You decide," he said. "You can stay here if you absolutely can't make yourself come out. But I need your help, and I am definitely not hiding from the Lost Books. *They* are hiding from *me*. And I am going to find them."

19

"And then he said," her brother said, lowering his voice, making it sound deeply ominous, "'*I am a librarian.*'" Charlie rolled his eyes. "As if any of us could ever forget it."

"You weren't even there talking to Miss Bug," Alex grumbled from over by a shelf of seedlings. He had paused to answer, and then started pacing again. "You were wedged into the passage, you muscle-bound lump."

They were in Kenneret's favorite place in the entire sprawling palace, especially in the wintertime—her greenhouse, a two-story glass building in the middle of the royal gardens. Like most people of Aethel, she loved plants and green, growing things. Some people cultivated roses, or exotic cactuses, or apricot and lemon trees in pots. All lovely, of course, but what she grew was vegetables. Ordinary potatoes, for example. Was there anything better than digging up a row of potatoes? Like hunting treasure in the dirt, she thought, better than gold. In her greenhouse she grew lettuces, leeks, cucumbers, and beets, and an herb garden with pale green sage, tiny thyme leaves, frondy parsley, and bulging heads of garlic.

Since becoming queen a few months ago, she hadn't had as much time to get dirt under her fingernails, but the steward had made sure that her greenhouse remained well heated, and the vegetables harvested and distributed in the poorer sections of the city.

Gardening made a nice excuse, too, for anyone who noticed the calluses on her fingers.

She couldn't weed and dig anymore, but she could take tea. She loved walking through the dormant garden outside, the ground frozen and hard, and stepping into the humid, warm air of the greenhouse, where she'd claimed a corner and had a simple wooden table set up, with chairs, and a stove with a kettle on it, and a tray of cakes and toast, teacups and a teapot.

Kenneret poured out tea, added a dollop of cream and a spoonful of sugar, and handed the cup to Charlie, who was still grinning at being called *muscle-bound*. "I do have a lot of muscles," he said confidingly.

"I've noticed," Kenneret said. "Alex, how do you like your tea?" she called.

He glanced toward the greenhouse door, as if he had somewhere else to be. "I don't want any." Then he stooped and pulled something from under a pot of parsley. A book, of all things. "What are *you* doing here?" she heard him mutter at the book as he stood, turning a few pages.

She turned to her brother. "So you like working for the royal librarian?"

"*Like* isn't exactly the word," Charlie said. "But it's interesting. I can see why he's so good at the sword."

"Why is that?" Kenneret asked. She kept an eye on Alex, who stood by the door, looking jittery.

"Focus," Charlie answered. "When you fight, you can't be distracted by anything, or worried about what's going to happen, you just . . ." He waved the knife he was using to butter a piece of toast, as if it were a sword. "Fight. He's the same way about being a librarian."

"Focused," Kenneret said.

"Yes," Charlie said, nodding. "If his pages didn't remind him, I think he'd forget to eat or sleep. I asked him to come out here for tea just now, but he didn't want to. 'Shut up and go away, Charlie' were his exact words."

Shooting Charlie a quelling look, Alex crossed their corner of the greenhouse and flung himself into a chair, where he set the book he'd been examining onto the table next to him. "Charlie," he said, nodding at her, "haven't you noticed that your sister is the same way about being queen?"

Kenneret choked on a sip of tea. He wasn't wrong. She was surprised, though, that he had noticed.

Charlie's grin widened. "Kennie, the only reason he left his precious library was because I told him that he needed to talk to you about what happened in the room with the weather books."

She nodded, and took a deep breath of the rich, earth-scented air. "I am concerned about it," she said with forced calm. "Is that kind of thing likely to happen again?"

"Yes." Alex leaned forward, putting his elbows on his knees. "Next time it's likely to be worse. It's because of the Lost Books. Book, in this case," he corrected himself. "I think." He frowned.

"Lost Books," she repeated. "That's new. Tell me what you know about them."

"I don't know much," he answered. "Librarians don't like passing along their secrets. Sixty years ago these Lost Books were made—they're books of power, made with magic. I don't know exactly how many of them there are, and I don't know enough about what they *do*. Sixty years ago, libraries were open, and people read books all the time. It's because of the Lost Books that libraries have been closed. At least one of them is hidden in the royal library." He gazed down at the damp slate floor of the greenhouse and rubbed his left wrist—something, Kenneret realized, that he did a lot. After a silent moment, he shot her a quick glance. "Kenneret, how well do you trust your uncle?"

She frowned at the change of subject. Four months ago she would have answered the question automatically. Now ... Uncle Patch had been behaving strangely, and he'd become so controlling. He was doing it, she felt sure, to protect her. "I trust him," she said slowly.

He nodded as if he'd expected her answer. "That's what I thought," he muttered. "He's the one who wrote to the duchess at Purslane, too?"

"Yes," she confirmed.

He rubbed his wrist some more, thinking. Then he shrugged and shot to his feet, as if he'd decided something. "The librarian's assistant that I met today, Miss Bug, is the one who told me about the Lost Book that is hidden in the royal library. Until we find it, it'll keep marking the other books, and the library itself will become even more deadly."

"Deadly?" Kenneret exclaimed. "It's just *books!*"

"I'm not exaggerating the danger," Alex said sharply. His hands, she noticed, were clenched.

"Why not just search the library, then?" Kenneret asked. "And find the Lost Book?"

He gave her one of his gray-eyed glares that was like being doused in icy water. "If it was that simple, *Your Majesty*, don't you think I would have done it already?"

"All right," she said. "So you're searching the library for this Lost Book. When you find it, will it be like that weather book with the mark on it?"

He wouldn't meet her eyes. "It'll probably be worse."

"I know what he's not telling you," Charlie put in, and took a slurp of his tea.

"Leave it, Charlie," Alex said sharply.

"Yesterday, in the weather room," her brother went on. "Did you notice, Kennie? All of the books, the marked one and the others, they all went after him." He nodded at Alex. "Not me, and not you. Him. *And* that other book attacked him, too." With a finger he drew a line on his face, in the same place that Alex had a scabbed line where he'd been cut by the marked book. "They don't like librarians, that's what I think."

Kenneret remembered something Alex had said at their very first meeting, in her office. "Ohhh. You think the previous royal librarian was killed by one of the marked books." Her heart gave a thump. "And your master at Purslane Castle?"

He frowned. "Yes."

"Why haven't they killed you?" Charlie asked.

"They've tried," Alex said darkly.

"Yeah, but why haven't they succeeded?" Charlie went on. "Are you special or something?"

Alex shot him an inimical glare, but Kenneret nodded. "He's right, Alex. You've admitted that you don't have much training. You're making this up as you go along, aren't you?" She met his level gaze. "So am I, to tell you the truth. But it means I have to ask: If the marked books are targeting librarians—killing them— how have you managed to stay alive this long?"

He was rubbing his wrist again. "I don't know."

Charlie rolled his eyes. "Sheer random chance? Blind luck? Your brilliance with the sword?" His face went suddenly serious. "Or maybe you're not really a librarian at all."

Kenneret thought Alex might burst into flames at

that. "I *am* a librarian," he bit out.

"I'm just saying," Charlie said, raising a hand, as if he'd just lost a point in sword practice. "Two librarians are dead, and you're not."

"Three librarians," Alex corrected him. "I got a letter the other day. The one at the Far Wrothing library was killed, too."

"*Three*," Kenneret exclaimed. "Alex! You're in terrible danger, aren't you?"

This was a lot more serious than she had realized. And Alex . . . she studied him. He *was* a librarian, she had no doubts about that. But he was Charlie's age. He'd admitted that he'd hardly apprenticed with the old librarian at Purslane Castle, and he didn't know the librarians' secrets. Clearly, despite his best intentions, the job was too big for him. "I think," she said slowly, "we need to call in reinforcements."

"More librarians," Alex said, nodding. "That's an excellent idea. I can write to the—"

"No," she interrupted. "We need soldiers to deal with this. I want to call in the Swift."

Alex blinked and stared at her, his face horrified.

"The Guardian of the North," Charlie put in, perking up. "Yes. That's just who we need." He nodded eagerly at Alex. "You should meet him, Alex. The Swift came to Starkcliffe one time. He's an amazing soldier and leader, one of the old nobility, so he's completely honorable and brave, and he—"

"No," Alex said suddenly, snatching up the book he'd taken from under the parsley pot. "Soldiers? Tromping all over my library with their big feet?"

"*Your* library?" Kenneret asked.

"My responsibility," he amended. She noticed that his knuckles were white where his hands were gripping the book. "Look, Kenneret, you can't fight this with swords." He paced toward the fogged-up windows, then back again.

"You used a sword before," Charlie put in.

"Shut up, Charlie," Alex muttered, still pacing.

Her corner of the greenhouse felt suddenly too small, not big enough to contain him. Coming to the windows, he turned and came back again, straight to her, where he held out the book. "Have you read this?"

She took the book and looked at the spine to see the title. *A Compendium of the Insect Species of the Itascan Subcontinental Region, Volume 13.*

"The Itascan subcontinent is thousands of miles away from this country," Alex pointed out. "Why is there a book about its insect species in here?"

She shook her head. "I have no idea. I have no interest in insects."

"Neither do I," Charlie put in.

Alex pointed at the book. "It should be in the library. It's like . . . it's like the library is extending its tentacles into the rest of the palace, and farther—even out here in the middle of the gardens. A soldier wouldn't know that this book is not supposed to be here. Not knowing that sort of thing could be very dangerous."

"Dangerous *how*, exactly?" Kenneret demanded.

He was gritting his teeth as he answered. "Yes, all right, fine. The marked books have only attacked me. *So far*. That doesn't mean other people aren't in danger, too. Anybody who opens a book to read it could be attacked. The library has to be kept locked up while I look for the Lost Book and figure out how to protect the books that haven't been marked yet, and put them back to sleep, if I can."

"To *sleep*?" she interrupted.

"The books are waking up. They're unsettled. Think of it this way, Kenneret. The marked books are the ones that are most awake. And a bunch of noisy, clod-footed soldiers are the last people we need messing around in there. They'll only make things worse."

Silently Kenneret held out the book about insects, and he stalked across the slate floor and took it from her hands. Alex had that ability to warp reality around him, to make what he wanted seem like the most logi-cal thing to do. But was it? Was it *really*?

She shook her head, decided. "We have to put an end to this," she said firmly. "I'm calling in the sol-diers. And we have a bit of luck on our side. Three of the Swift's men arrived at the palace this morning. I will send them—"

"They're *here*?" Alex interrupted.

"Yes," Kenneret said, and continued. "As I was say-ing, I will send them back to the Swift at once with a message to bring more soldiers, well armed. He can be here within a few days, I should think. I will have them dismantle the library."

"*Dismantle?*" he said sharply.

"Yes." She nodded. "And if necessary, they will burn the Lost Book and the books that have been marked."

His face went stark white. "*Burn* the books?"

"I know the library is important to you, Alex, but—"

"Kenneret, it's the *library*," he said wildly. "You can't destroy it."

"Oh, can't I?" She leaned forward, gripping the arms of her chair. "Have you forgotten, Alex? I am the queen. *We* are the queen."

"So what does *that* mean?" His voice was bitter. "That you get to do whatever you want?"

"No," she shot back. "Being queen does not mean

doing whatever I want. It means that I'm the one who has to make the hard decisions."

"You're making the wrong decision this time." His eyes blazed with fury. "I'm a librarian, and I will *not* let you destroy my library."

Before she could reply to that outrageous statement, he whirled and stormed out of the greenhouse, slamming the door behind him so hard that the teacups rattled in their saucers and the fronds of the seedlings trembled.

She sat staring at the door, her heart pounding, still gripping the arms of her chair. He wouldn't *let* her? How . . . how dare he?

"Well, *that* was interesting," Charlie said. He was slathering butter onto another piece of toast. His face was blank again. It meant, Kenneret had figured out, that he was thinking hard.

"What was interesting?" she asked, taking a deep breath to steady herself. "Alex getting mad? It seems to be his usual state. It's not the first time he's slammed a door on his way out."

"He wasn't mad," Charlie said through a bite of toast. "He was terrified."

"What?" She blinked, surprised. Then she nodded, realizing. "He knows that the marked books want to kill him."

"Nope." Charlie took a swig of tea. "That's not what he's afraid of." He set down his cup. "Let me tell you something, Kennie. I'm reckoned to be pretty good at the sword. Hardly anybody at Starkcliffe could give me any trouble. You saw my duel with Alex. It lasted about ten seconds because he is way, way better than I am. The best I've ever seen, actually. You don't get to be that good at the sword without working at it."

She knew that, of course.

"Good fighters train every day, for years," Charlie went on. As proof, he held out his hand and pointed at the white scars that crossed his knuckles.

Alex, she knew, had the same scars on the back of his hand. "Oh," she breathed. "So . . . you think Alex was trained to be a soldier?"

"Not only that," Charlie said. "Did you see his face when you mentioned the Swift?" When she nodded, he went on. "You've met the Swift before, right?"

"Yes, of course," Kenneret replied. The Swift was one of the most powerful people in the kingdom, and an important advisor to the queen, though he'd been distracted by family matters, or so his letter had said, so he had not had time to meet with her since she'd become queen. As the Guardian of the North, the Swift had a fortress near the border, where his main duty was to keep the Greylings from raiding the farms and sheepfolds of that part of the kingdom. He was very tall and had the rich, brown skin and dark eyes of the old nobility, and a scar across his forehead; he was loud, as if he was used to shouting orders at people, and he was rather terrifyingly competent. A leader who did not put up with any nonsense. Everything she'd heard about the Swift made her inclined to like him, but whether they could work together remained to be seen.

Charlie leaned forward. "I asked Alex who taught him the sword and he got all snippy about it. I think he was probably one of the Swift's Family. It's this elite group of soldiers that are specially chosen to live with the Swift at his fortress, and train there."

"I know about the Family, Charlie," she reminded him.

"Right, well. I'm guessing that Alex ran away from them. I think he's a deserter. That's why he's so afraid. The Swift demands absolute loyalty from his chosen ones. If they catch up with him, Alex will be in a lot of trouble." His face grew suddenly serious. "*When* they catch up to him, I mean. A *lot* of trouble."

20

Well, he'd pretty much blasted everything into pieces so tiny he'd never find them all.

Alex left the queen's greenhouse, following the paths through the gardens and into the palace, his hands jammed in his coat pockets, the book under his arm. Instead of going straight back to the library, he walked off his temper, scowling at the floor as he wandered the halls.

The business with the soldiers, and all of that—it was bad enough.

But worse—far worse—was Kenneret's plan to burn the marked books. *Yes* they were dangerous, and *yes* the Lost Book behind it all was surely even more dangerous, but burning? No.

Didn't she understand what it meant to be a librarian? All of the books were alive, in a strange bookish way. But it was like Miss Bug had said. The books didn't *do*. They didn't act. *He* had to act for them. He had to protect the books that hadn't been marked, *and* try to save the ones that had. That was a librarian's true purpose.

He wasn't sure how he was going to manage it. He had to find the Lost Book and prevent the marked books from attacking him while saving the library and all the other books before the soldiers arrived.

And Charlie hadn't been wrong about the marked weather book attacking him specifically. *They don't like librarians*, Charlie had said.

Charlie, who was just as clever, in his own way, as his older sister, even though he couldn't read. He'd seen straight through to the truth of it. For some reason, the Lost Books hated librarians. Hated him, Alex, in particular. Why? He wanted to protect the books, not harm them!

And then there was Lord Patch, who was clearly searching for the Lost Book. Why did he want it? Alex had no idea. And he couldn't cast any doubt on Patch, because, as Kenneret said, she trusted her uncle.

He frowned and kept walking, and realized, with a start, that he was rubbing his wrist. Because it itched. He stopped in the middle of a dim hallway, pulled up his sleeve, and sure enough, the letters were shifting. After a moment they settled into a word.

CODEX

"I have no idea what that means," he said aloud.

The letters jumbled again, and re-formed.

CODEX

"Thank you very much," he said acidly to the mark on his wrist, and started walking again. "So helpful. A codex is a book. I already *know* that."

And—oh, wonderful. Perfect! As if things couldn't get any better!—more trouble was waiting for him outside the door of the library.

Two of the Swift's Family, in sleek black uniforms, armed with the best swords and daggers.

They were playing Flinch, that stupid game that tested their reflexes and left the slower of the pair with bruised knuckles.

Tall, redheaded Jeffen was the first one to spot him as he came along the hallway. "Look who it is!" he exclaimed, jumping to his feet.

"Alex!" It was long, lanky Franciss, her short black hair sticking up like a bristly brush on her head. "We missed you like a toothache!"

They were both grinning like lunatics.

"Aren't you glad to see us, kid?" Jeffen asked as Alex stepped past them.

"Overjoyed," Alex said grimly, and pulled out the key to the library door. He hoped they couldn't see that his hands were shaking. "Aren't there supposed to be three of you?"

"You just missed Perryn," Jeffen said cheerfully. "He was summoned to the queen not five minutes ago."

Alex nodded and unlocked the door. Kenneret would send Perryn straight to the fortress with a message. She really was calling for soldiers. Or for the Family, at least.

"So it's just us two to keep you company until the Swift gets here," Jeffen said, following Alex into the library, Franciss a step behind him.

"To keep an eye on me, you mean," Alex said. He tried to keep his voice even, but his heart was pounding. "So he knows I'm here?"

"Yep. He's on his way." Jeffen stood in the middle of the main room looking around at what, the day before, the queen had called a *disaster*. Stacks of books everywhere, cards and scraps of paper strewn about, the map laid out on the floor, dust and cobwebs. "Nice place you've got here, kid."

He didn't bother replying. They made no secret of the fact that they thought books were not only snaky and weird, but boring, too. Why read, Jeffen would say, when you could use the time to practice your sword technique?

"We've been looking for you for months," Jeffen said, suddenly serious. "You're slippery, Alex. Now that we've got you, we're not letting you get away from us."

"I'm not going anywhere," Alex said, just as serious. "I'm a librarian."

Franciss snorted.

Jeffen cast him a skeptical look. "Oh, *sure* you are."

Of course they didn't believe him. Any more than his father would, when he arrived at the palace. He swallowed down a familiar lump of despair. "So how did you find me?"

"We stopped at that inn," Jeffen answered. He stepped around a pile of books that hadn't been there when Alex had left earlier. "Where was it again, Fran?"

Franciss had gone to crouch by the map, where she reached out to turn a corner of it to see better. "Pur-something," she replied.

"Don't touch anything," Alex put in.

Raising her eyebrows, Franciss got gracefully to her feet and wiped dusty fingertips on the front of her uniform.

"Purslane, right," Jeffen went on. "A boy at the inn there told us that you said you were heading west, Alex. Knowing you, we figured that meant you'd gone east. Wasn't much of a challenge after that to track you down to the Winter Palace."

"Why'd he send you two?" Alex asked. "He wanted to get rid of you?"

"Hah!" Jeffen laughed. "The kid hasn't lost his edge, has he?" he asked Franciss.

"He's all edge, really," she answered. She hopped up to sit on the reading table, her long legs swinging. "He's as sharp as a . . . a sharp thing."

"If Alex was a weapon, what would he be?" Jeffen said, lounging in a chair and resting his booted feet on another chair.

Alex gritted his teeth and set down the insect book he'd taken from Kenneret's room. The Family loved conversations like this. In a minute they'd be talking about where to get the best steel, or arguing about how to fight somebody who had a longer reach than you did.

"If the Swift was a weapon, he'd be a broadsword," Jeffen said.

"No, a double-headed ax," Franciss disagreed. "What d'you think, Alex?"

"No idea," he replied. Leaving the book on the

table, he went to the map and crouched there, looking it over and trying not to let himself be drawn into their conversation.

"Or a war hammer, maybe," Jeffen said with a shrug. "But Alex, he'd be a knife."

Franciss nodded. "Wickedly sharp."

"Coated with acid," Jeffen said, "so you don't even know that you've been cut until all of a sudden you realize that you're dead."

"If you're dead," Alex put in, annoyed, "you can't realize anything."

"That's true," Franciss said.

"In the moment before you're dead, then," Jeffen reasoned.

Alex gritted his teeth and looked over the map. He'd missed the Family so much during the past few months that he'd forgotten how some of them made him completely *crazy*.

"Any chance of us getting some dinner?" Franciss asked.

Still crouching by the map, Alex turned to say something cutting, when he saw Jeffen lean across the table, pick up the book Alex had left there, and open it. At the same moment, he saw the symbol of the Lost Book scorch into the cover, outlined in an ember-bright flame.

Alex leaped to his feet. "I told you not to touch—"

"Gah!" Jeffen shrieked, staring at the first page. "Ants!"

A heartbeat later, a hundred black ants the size of a thumb swarmed out of the pages.

"Close the book!" Alex snapped.

Jeffen howled and dropped the book, which lay open on the table. Ants boiled out of it. He backed away, his eyes wide. "Gah!"

Franciss jumped off the table and whipped out her sword.

The ants scurried out onto the table, and then seemed to get their bearing. They ignored the two soldiers. With the *scritch-scritch* sound of a thousand tiny legs, they flowed into an attack on Alex.

In one bound, Alex left the map, crossed the floor, and dove, sliding on his belly across the surface of the table, the ants crawling all over him, and seized the book. The symbol burned under his fingers. A second later, he snapped the book shut. A creepy sensation prickled over his skin, and the ants were crawling up his sleeves and down the collar of his coat. With a yell, still holding the book closed, he rolled off the table, feeling ant bodies squishing underneath him.

"Get it off!" Jeffen shouted, and then Franciss was

dragging him to his feet, unbuttoning his coat, and pulling it off him.

Feeling the sting of tiny bites on his arms, Alex kept a tight grip on the book and leaned against the table, shaking, while Franciss and Jeffen brushed him off and stamped on all the ants.

"Pages!" he croaked, and a moment later his pages flocked around him, ready to obey his orders. "Box," he told them. "And padlock." As the book writhed in his hands, he flung an order at Franciss. "Give me your dagger."

She stamped on another ant, pulled a dagger out of a sheath at her belt, and tossed it to him, hilt-first. He caught it, set down the squirming book, and stabbed it straight through, the dagger biting deep into the table, pinning the book closed. It buzzed and chittered, fighting to get free.

"Hurry up!" Alex shouted. A second later, four pages swooped over them, dropping a metal box that landed with a *thud* on the tabletop; two more brought a padlock. As Jeffen shook out Alex's coat, and Franciss stomped on the rest of the ants scurrying around on the floor, Alex transferred the insect book into the box, pulled the dagger out of it, slammed the cover closed, and locked it.

Staying quiet, Alex held the dagger out to Franciss, who took it with a nod. He inspected a few swelling ant bites on the skin of his arm. With a shrug, he started pulling on his shabby velvet coat.

"So," Jeffen said. "You're the librarian here?"

"Yes." Alex pulled the ring of keys out of his coat pocket and added the key to the padlock. "Royal librarian."

"He's not going to like it," Jeffen warned.

Alex released a shaking breath. "Yeah, I know. But that's the least of my problems." He pointed at the metal box that was holding the insect book. "Until about half an hour ago, that was in the queen's greenhouse. What do you think would have happened if *she'd* opened it?"

21

With a bolt of cold horror, Alex realized the significance of what he'd just said.

Up to now, the marked books had only attacked librarians. Jeffen, Alex knew, was barely even a reader, yet the book on insect species had been activated when *he* opened it.

There might be books like that hidden all over the palace. *Any* book could be burned with the Lost Books symbol and turned into a weapon. Everyone in the palace might be in danger.

For just a second, he felt a prickle of panic. Kenneret had been right. This was all too much for him to manage.

He knew what his pa would say. *One thing at a time, son.*

Alex took a steadying breath. The thing his pa valued most wasn't excellence with weapons, or bravery in battle, or anything like that; it was *competence.* The ability to get things done.

Right. No panic.

He would get this done.

"Page!" Alex shouted.

A second later, he was surrounded by pages, thirty of them at least. They were all trembling, as if they were frightened. "Two of you go and fetch my sword from my office," he ordered, putting the key ring into his coat pocket. "And two more, go find Miss Bug. She's probably still hiding in her cave."

"What about us?" Jeffen asked, getting to his feet. Franciss was at his shoulder; she gave a brisk nod.

Alex considered them. Another thing his pa had taught him from the time he'd been a tiny kid was leadership. A good leader gave orders and all of that, but the most important thing he or she had to do was choose good, *competent* people to give them to. Being part of the Family was like having twenty intensely annoying older brothers and sisters. Who, apart from the occasional bug-related panic, all happened to be extremely well-trained fighters.

"I could use your help," Alex admitted.

"Hah!" Jeffen exclaimed. "You hear that, Fran?"

"Yep," she said, grinning. "Loud and clear as mud!"

Two of Alex's pages swooped up and dropped his sheathed sword on the table. He belted it on and picked up the metal box. "I have to deal with this first." Inside the box, the insect book buzzed, and there was a scrabbling noise coming from it like lots of tiny legs trying to escape. "Jeffen, wait here for Miss Bug."

"Bug?" Jeffen asked, casting a dubious look at the box.

"She's harmless," Alex said. "At least, I'm pretty sure she is. Franciss, you're with me." He started toward the spiral stairs that led to the fourth level and headed up, Franciss a step behind him.

As they reached the balcony at the fourth level, Alex heard a muffled *thump-thump-thump*. "Light," he muttered, and a moment later, a page darted up with a light-well. He peered down the dim, book-lined hallway the noise was coming from. A door at the far end was blocked with sandbags. The blackpowder explosions book was in there, he remembered. Behind the barricade, the door was shaking. The book was trying to escape. But it had been padlocked to its shelf, Alex was certain.

"What is it?" Franciss asked, peering over his shoulder.

Alex swallowed. "Dangerous book. I can't deal with it right now." He'd just have to hope the door stayed locked and the sandbag barricade held. "Come on."

He started around the fourth-floor balcony, then stopped.

"What?" Franciss asked.

He shook his head and held up a hand for quiet. At the same moment, the letters on his wrist gave a warning prickle.

The light-well was a faint glow at his shoulder. Night had fallen—it was nearly dark outside the grimy windows of the library. From down near the floor came another glow, the light he'd left with Jeffen. The rest of the huge room was filled with shadows. And with something else. *Fear.*

All the books—every single one of them—were trembling on their shelves.

Gah. He knew what this meant for them. It went beyond the fear he'd felt coming from them before. Now they were terrified. Of what? They knew the Lost Book's power was growing, that they were all running out of time. "Sorry," he said aloud. His voice echoed in the wide room. *Sorry, sorry, sorry.*

"Who're you talking to?" Franciss whispered.

"The books," Alex said. He spoke louder. "I'll do whatever I can to protect you," he promised them. Then he checked his wrist.

The word **CODEX** was gone. It had been replaced with a new word. **KEYS**. "Yes," he said aloud. "Thank you. That's what I thought."

Franciss was giving him a strange look.

"Yeah, I know," he said to her, and continued around the balcony. The books here were even more uneasy; the air shivered with their fright. Alex led Franciss down the hallway that led to the fortress room where he'd been storing the marked books. Six of them were in there, all locked into boxes, and the room itself was secured with a bolt and two padlocks.

When they got to it, the door was shuddering under an assault from within. Alex heard a crash of thunder, and a puddle of water seeped out from the crack under the door. The weather book was definitely loose. There was a faint *thump-thump, thump-thump* sound— the heart book had gotten out of its box, too.

And one of the padlocks on the door was hanging open. Unlocked.

"What's in there?" Franciss asked.

"What do you think?" Alex said sharply.

"Books?" Franciss's eyes widened.

"Really dangerous ones," Alex said. "And the locks won't hold them for much longer." What to do with the insect book in its metal box? He didn't have any time to waste. Quickly he pulled out his key ring, then handed the box to Franciss. "When I open the door, you toss that inside, all right?"

Franciss gave a brisk nod.

Trying to keep his hands from shaking, Alex inserted the key and unlocked the padlock. Then he pulled back the bolt. "Ready?" he asked.

"Ready."

He jerked the door open, and Franciss hurled the metal box containing the ant book into the room.

Alex put his shoulder to the door, but it wouldn't budge. Peering through the crack, he saw four marked books unchained and unboxed, all pushing against him. "Help!"

Franciss leaped to obey, adding her strength to his. In a whirl of white, Alex's pages joined them, plastering themselves against the door. Another moment of struggle, and the door slammed closed.

"Hold it," Alex gasped, and threw the bolt. Then he put on both padlocks and locked them both securely.

It might hold for a little while, anyway.

His pages slid to the floor, as if exhausted.

"No time to rest," he told them, and they picked

themselves up again. "Come on," he said to Franciss, who had a hand on her sword, ready to draw it. "We need to hurry."

They raced down to the ground floor, trailed by a cloud of Alex's pages.

When they got there they found Miss Bug perched on a chair at one of the reading tables, her face pale, her eyes huge behind her thick spectacles, her two pages trembling at her shoulder. Jeffen stood nearby.

As Alex hurried up, Jeffen joked, "You're only *pretty sure* she's harmless?"

Ignoring him, Alex stalked straight up to Miss Bug. "You didn't tell me everything you knew before. You'd better tell me now."

She blinked.

"No more secrets." He pointed toward the fourth level. "I've been having trouble with the locks to this place since the day I got here. Now the marked books are getting out of securely locked boxes. One of the Lost Books has already been found, hasn't it?"

She blinked again.

"You are *not* incompetent," he growled at her. "Don't pretend to be. You told me one of the Lost Books was written by a *whatsit with the locks*. A locksmith?"

"A thief," she said, in a thready voice. "A lockpick."

"What's it called?" Alex demanded.

"The Keys Treatise," Bug answered.

"Keys, right, of course," Alex muttered. So the word **KEYS** on his wrist had been what, a warning? "And anybody who has read the Keys Treatise has the power to open any lock, is that it?"

Miss Bug nodded, her eyes wide.

"The Keys Treatise must have been found months ago. But it's not the only Lost Book in this library." Alex bent down closer so he could look straight into Miss Bug's big eyes. "And the other Lost Book is the one that was written by a king, isn't it? The *self* of a king is trapped in it?"

"The Scroll of Kings, yes," Bug answered. Her bony hands were clenched together.

"Somebody's been looking for it," Alex said.

Bug's wizened face crinkled in dismay. "The one who reads it can use its power." Then she shook her head, whispering to herself, "No, no, that's not quite it." She blinked up at Alex again. "The reader can *command* its power."

Alex straightened. He tried to ignore the fact that Jeffen and Franciss were staring at him, and so was Bug. "Lord Patch has been searching the library for the Scroll of Kings," he said slowly. And *why* had he been searching for it all this time?

The next thought hit Alex like a blow from a war hammer. It practically made his ears ring.

Lord Patch wanted the throne—he wanted to rule, as king. When he found the Scroll he would use it to go after Kenneret.

22

Even with everything going on in the royal library, Kenneret still had other queenly duties. Usually she worked late into the night in her office by herself, with two guards outside the door, and a secretary ready to come in to take notes if she needed him, and another servant waiting to bring tea if she wanted it. Tonight Charlie had insisted on staying with her.

Her brother, she knew, was worried about Alex, and was probably trying to figure out a way to make sure he didn't get into too much trouble when the Swift arrived.

"Kennie," he began.

"No," she interrupted, without looking up from her notes.

"You don't even know what I was going to say," he complained.

"Yes, I did. You were going to ask me to intercede with the Swift so Alex doesn't get into trouble." She gave her brother a raised-eyebrows look. "Weren't you?"

He rubbed his chin with the thinking-mitten. "Yes," he admitted.

"Charlie," she said patiently. "You know very well that I can't do that."

"But you're the queen," he protested.

"All the more reason." She dipped her pen into the inkpot. "The Family is the Swift's business, not mine. I can't meddle."

"Yeah, I know," Charlie said morosely.

Kenneret worked on, surrounded by a bubble of light from a brace of candles on her desk. With quick pen strokes she took notes, paused to read, then took more notes. The cushion on her chair was as uncomfortable as it ever was.

Charlie fell asleep, snoring loudly, and then snuffled and snorted and turned onto his side. Then his snoring stopped.

In the sudden quiet, Kenneret put down the pen and stretched.

Then she froze.

The flames at the ends of the candles on her desk were shivering. Something was disturbing them. She felt a trembling in the air, and heard a faint rustling noise.

A mouse?

Slowly she got to her feet.

The noise, she realized, had woken Charlie—she could see his eyes gleaming in the candlelight. He sat up on the couch, staring at her.

No, *past* her.

"What is it?" she whispered.

"Behind you, Kennie," he whispered back.

Her heart started to beat faster. Her desk faced the office door; behind it, behind her chair, were shelves of . . . not books, exactly—not something anyone would ever read. They were there mostly for show; she wasn't even sure what they were about. Dull reports on grain production, she thought, maybe, or tax records. They covered the entire wall, each one bound in brown leather, its title stamped in gold.

"Alex said they only attack librarians, right?" Charlie asked, still whispering.

Kenneret's hands went to her desk drawer; she slid it open and pulled out the sleek dagger she kept there. If only she had a sword . . .

Charlie had gotten to his feet. "Kennie, I think you'd better come over here," he whispered.

With the dagger clenched in her hand, she slid around the desk, and in three gliding steps was across the room next to Charlie, where she whirled to face the shelves.

The things that, maybe, were books after all, were vibrating.

A second later, they were bumping and thumping against their shelves, with a sound like a thousand running footsteps.

The thumping steadied until they were all banging the shelves in unison, loud enough that Kenneret wanted to put her hands over her ears.

Instead she gripped the knife, ready to defend herself, and her brother.

"What's going on?" Charlie shouted.

"I don't know!"

Then she heard the door bang open—and at the same moment, she realized what the books were doing. It was an ambush. She whirled, knowing who she'd see in the doorway. "Alex!" she shouted. "Duck!"

He didn't hesitate—thank goodness, she thought in a flash, he knew how to take an order—dropping to the floor as five heavy books—yes, they *were* books—all blazing with the Lost Books symbol, hurtled through the air like cannonballs, passing just over Alex's head and slamming into the wall in the passageway outside her office.

"Yipes," Charlie gasped.

The books started thumping again. A soldier dressed in black was already dragging Alex out of the doorway. "Come on!" he shouted, leaping into the office, seizing Kenneret's arm, and hustling her out of the room. Charlie followed, and the door slammed behind them. The air felt suddenly clearer. Kenneret took a gasping breath.

The hallway was crowded with Alex, just getting to his feet, her brother, the black-clad soldier—a member of the Swift's Family, she realized—and her own guards.

The tax records and grain production reports that had attacked Alex lay in a tumbled heap against the wall of the passageway. A few pages stirred, as if there was a breeze. Which there wasn't. The pile shifted.

From inside her office came the sound of a rumbling crash, as if the entire shelf had just collapsed. It was followed by a *thump-thump-thump* that rattled the door in its frame. The books, trying to escape.

No. They were trying to get at Alex.

His face was grim as he stepped closer to her and bent to peer into her eyes. "Where is your uncle?"

It was such an unexpected question. She shook her head. "I don't know. It's late. I expect he's in his rooms. He—"

"No, he's not," Alex interrupted, looking deadly serious. "Listen, Kenneret. Your Majesty, I mean. Since the day I got here, your uncle has been trying to get rid of me. He sent that letter to Purslane, and I'm pretty sure he told your steward to offer me money to leave, and I'm betting he's been working on you, too, telling you how inexperienced I am, that I'm too young for the job, and all of that."

"Maybe he simply doesn't like you, Alex," she reasoned.

"No," he said quickly. "I mean, yes, he doesn't like me, but that isn't it. He was searching for one of the Lost Books, and he didn't want me making his search more difficult."

"But you're just a librarian," Charlie blurted out.

"Charlie," Alex said, his voice positively dripping acid, "I pretty much want to kill you right now. A librarian is never *just* a librarian. And the Lost Books are far more than just books."

Kenneret shook her head. "But why would Uncle Patch want to find one of the Lost Books?"

"Why do you think?" Alex asked sharply.

Her eyes widened. He couldn't be suggesting . . .

From her office came the sound of glass shattering.

"Uh, sorry to interrupt," said the black-clad soldier. "But I'm not sure that door is going to hold." He pointed at Kenneret's office. Then he pointed at the pile of books that had attacked before. "And those ones are looking restless . . ."

"Yes, of course," Kenneret said. "You two"—she pointed at her guards—"stay here and make sure the books don't escape, or come after us." Leaving them to it, she turned and started walking down the hallway.

Alex took two quick steps to catch up with her. "Your Majesty, your uncle has found at least one of the Lost Books. It's called the Keys Treatise, and it gives its reader the power to unlock any door. I think he's been using the Treatise to search the library for another Lost Book, one called the Scroll of Kings. It was written by a legendary king, and whoever reads it gains great power."

Charlie was a step behind her, followed by the black-clad Family soldier. "What power?" he asked, as the sound of the books pounding on her office door faded.

When Alex answered, his voice sounded bleak. "The power to rule."

She couldn't bring herself to believe what he was suggesting. Her uncle had done his best to raise her and Charlie—well, he'd sent Charlie away to school, but he'd always been there for her, as her regent, and then as an advisor. He had tried to counsel her, pointing out whenever she made stupid mistakes or bad decisions. Maybe . . . maybe he had done that because he wanted her to fail.

Had he been undermining her all along? He was so hard to read—he always presented a bland, smiling face to the world. "This Keys Treatise," she asked Alex, who paced at her side. "You think it was found four months ago?"

"Yeah, about that long, I'm guessing," Alex answered. "Look, Kennie, we don't—"

She held up a hand, and he fell silent. Her brother, a step behind them, was listening.

It had been four months since her uncle had changed. She had wondered why—and now she knew. That's when he had found the Lost Book. "If the Keys Treatise was found," she asked Alex, "and read, would the person who read it learn about the Scroll of Kings?"

He nodded. "Yes. I think he would."

Kenneret took a few more steps, then stopped. The others gathered around her. Saying it aloud would make it real, and true. "My uncle is making a bid for the throne," she said slowly. "He wants to rule Aethel." She closed her eyes for half a second, feeling a wash of fear, and betrayal, and sorrow, too, that her uncle could do such a thing. But she was queen. She could not give in to those feelings. She would grieve later; she would be furious later. Right now she had to act. She had to *be queen*.

When she opened her eyes again, she was all grim purpose. "All right," she rapped out. "My uncle knows that the Scroll of Kings can give him the power to get rid of me and take the throne. He has been searching for it for months. Do you think he has found it?"

As an answer, Alex held up his hand, then pushed up his sleeve to reveal his wrist. He was wearing a bracelet of some kind—no, it was a tattoo. He held it closer, turning his hand so she could see better.

In dark letters against the pale skin of his wrist was a single word.

KINGS

She looked up, meeting Alex's gray eyes. "What does that mean?"

"It's a warning, Your Majesty," Alex answered promptly. "It means that he's either found the Scroll, or he's about to."

"All right," she snapped. "How do we stop him?"

23

"Lord Patch has to be in the library somewhere," Alex said.

"Then we'll go to the library," Kenneret said steadily, "and we'll find him." She set off down the mirrored, gilded hallway. Alex fell in beside her. Charlie was a step behind, with Jeffen.

They hurried around a corner. "Thanks for coming with me," Alex panted as they sprinted up a marble stairway lit only by a fading light-well in a sconce.

"I'm not," Kenneret answered briskly. "*You* are coming with *me*. We'll deal with my uncle together, and with the Scroll of Kings."

Alex frowned, knowing what she meant by *dealing with* the Lost Book.

Kenneret looked over her shoulder at Jeffen, two steps below them. "The Swift and the rest of the Family were already on their way here, and they will arrive very soon. Possibly even by morning. Do you think we can hold out until then?"

"What," Alex said shortly, "so you can have them dismantle and burn the library?"

"I will do what has to be done," she replied.

The thought of that possibility made his head spin. He would die before he let it happen. He knew she intended to burn the Scroll of Kings, too, if she got her hands on it. The Lost Books could be used by evil people for evil purposes, but the books themselves were *not* evil, he was sure of it. They contained the self of a person—they were *alive*—and they didn't deserve to be burned. There was an alternative. He just had to figure out what it was.

As they reached the top of the stairs, Charlie took two quick steps to hurry at Alex's other side. "Listen," he said. "Once this is over, assuming we're all still alive, I can help you get away. I know some good hiding places."

Alex glanced aside. "Get away? From who?"

"*The Family*," Charlie hissed in a voice loud enough for the other two to hear. "And the Swift. They're going to arrest you."

Alex blinked. "Arrest me? No they're not."

"But you ran away from the Swift's fortress, didn't you?" Charlie asked.

"Last time I checked," Alex said sharply, starting to lose his patience, "running away from home wasn't a crime."

"From . . . from home?" Charlie and Kenneret exchanged a glance.

Alex was definitely not going to explain it all now, and anyway, they'd reached the remote hallway with the worn carpet that led to the library door. It was time for action.

Taking out his key ring, he unlocked the library door, and they all trooped in.

They found Bug and Franciss huddled under one of the long wooden reading tables. Scattered all around it were books sprawled with their covers open, tumbled over each other.

High above, on the third-floor balcony, a book slid off its shelf, plunged through the air, and Alex stepped aside as it slammed into the place he'd been standing.

"They keep doing that," Franciss said, crawling out

from under the table, casting a wary look at the book-shelves. "Attacking us!" Bug stayed where she was, her big eyes blinking.

Alex bent and picked up the book. It was a history of naval battles, and it was trembling. "What's the matter?" he asked, unbending a few pages and closing the book, smoothing the cover with his fingers. He shook his head. That hadn't been an attack.

"He talks to the books," he heard Franciss whisper to the others.

"They're afraid," he said. "They know something is wrong, and they're trying to get away." Looking up, he saw rank on rank of bookshelves, the balconies and catwalks, the shadowed ceiling high above. Every book was terrified; the air shivered with it. They knew the entire library was in danger—from burning, dis-mantling, from being marked by the Lost Books, from Patch's plans. He didn't have much time. The mark on his wrist meant that Patch had found the Scroll of Kings. He was probably reading it now. The longer they waited, the more likely he was to finish it and command its power.

But they couldn't rush into this fight. His pa had taught him that whenever a leader went into battle, he or she had to consider the objectives of the fight, the resources at hand, and the enemy.

The objective, of course, was to save the books.

And the queen.

His pa would have something to say about the order of importance there. But Alex was not the Swift, he was a librarian, and for him the books came first, always.

He bent to check under the table. Miss Bug peered back at him. "Are you going to hide or help?" he asked her.

She blinked three times and hunched her thin shoulders.

"It's for the library," he added, and reached out a hand to her.

Her bug eyes squinted at his hand. She leaned closer. "What is *that*?"

Her twiglike finger pointed at the bracelet of letters on his left wrist. The word **KINGS** was still printed there.

Miss Bug was staring at him, and her lips were moving. "You . . . are . . . marked . . ." she whispered.

He didn't have time to explain what had happened all those years ago with the Red Codex in his father's library. "Are you coming out or not?" he asked impatiently.

"All right," she said in her high voice, and started crawling out from under the table.

As he straightened, another book plummeted from a high shelf.

"Yipes!" Charlie said, and leaped out of its way, and it crashed to the floor next to him.

Alex surveyed the others. Jeffen and Franciss: well armed and well trained, and they would take his orders. Charlie: had his sword. Bug: a librarian, but maybe not of much use. His pages would do as they were told, but they were simple creatures. They couldn't do much.

And Kenneret? She was short and snub-nosed, and she wasn't even wearing her crown, and she was completely self-possessed as she returned his speculative look with a calm gaze of her own. The queen was beyond competent. She was an equal ally in this fight. Alex felt fairly certain that her uncle had underestimated her strength.

And now, the enemy. "Lord Patch is in the library somewhere," Alex told them. "He has just found the Scroll of Kings, and he's reading it, which means he'll soon gain the power of a king, if he doesn't have it already. We have to find him, and take the Scroll."

"And burn it," Kenneret added.

He shot her a glare.

"It's dangerous," she reasoned.

"And evil," Miss Bug piped up.

"Books are not evil," Alex told them, and not for the first time, either. Shaking his head, he set aside the argument. "The question is, where is Lord Patch hiding?" Dodging another falling book that crashed down behind him, he went to look at the map of the library, which was laid out in the middle of the stone floor. It was a sprawling mess, really, with extra pages tacked onto its edges where he'd found new rooms and corridors, secret tunnels, stairways, trapdoors, Miss Bug's little cave, the barricaded room where the blackpowder explosions book was stored, and the other fortified room where he'd locked up the marked books. It was a true maze on five different levels. They could easily get lost in it, and Patch knew it as well as he did—or better.

As he'd found each book marked with the Lost Books symbol, he'd put an X on the map, but there was no pattern to it—at least, not one that he could see. Standing, he walked around to the other side of the map and crouched again, trying to puzzle it out.

Dimly he was aware of other books falling from the shelves, a distant banging sound, which, he guessed, was the marked books trying to escape from the fortified room, and of Jeffen and Franciss with hands on their swords, ready for action, and Kenneret talking to Miss Bug.

"The king who wrote the Scroll of Kings," the queen asked. "Was he a good king? Do you know?"

Miss Bug's whispery voice answered. "He was. He

was from far away and not from Aethel, but he was good. A bad, evil book, but a good king."

"I see," Kenneret said musingly, as if she was thinking.

Studying the map, Alex shook his head. No, he couldn't figure it out. He got to his feet. "All right," he started. "We'll have to—"

"Wait a minute," Charlie interrupted.

"We don't have a minute," Alex snapped.

"Ten seconds," Charlie amended, still gazing at the map. And as Alex stared at him in astonishment, the prince climbed onto a chair and then onto the reading table. He ducked as a book whizzed past his head, and then he shot Alex a triumphant grin. "There *is* a pattern. You just can't see it from down there. Look!"

Alex scrambled onto the table and looked, and sure enough, Charlie was right. From a height, the pattern left by the marked books was obvious, one *X* leading to another, to another, forming the shape of the Lost Books symbol, all leading to . . . "There," Alex said, pointing. A room on the fifth floor, in the deepest depths of the library. "That's where he is." The room where the Scroll of Kings had been hidden—the room where they'd find Lord Patch.

24

"Come on!" Alex ordered. Jumping off the table, he started across the stone floor. With Kenneret and Charlie a step behind him, he climbed up the spiral staircase; Jeffen and Franciss, with Miss Bug scurrying along between them, brought up the rear.

As they reached the second level, a rumbling roar echoed through the big main room of the library.

"What was *that?*" Jeffen cried, putting his hand on his sword.

Alex paused and consulted his mental map of the library. "Zoological books are down there." Books about all kinds of animals. "A marked book about lions, probably."

"Lions!" cried Jeffen.

"Or tigers," Alex said grimly, and kept going up the stairs. From the corner of his eye he caught a glimpse of a huge, tawny shape bursting from a passageway on the ground level and bounding across the stone floor, heading for the stairs. Another echoing roar filled the room.

"It's a lion, all right!" Jeffen shouted.

"Keep going," Alex panted, and they pounded up the spiral stairs. As they went around the curve, he caught another glimpse of the lion bounding up the stairs after them, and then they were past the second-floor balcony, headed for the third.

From down another passageway on the other side of the main room came a hissing sound.

"Oh, please, let it not be snakes," he heard Jeffen gasp, and then a torrent of steel-tipped arrows burst out of a doorway and shot across the library, aimed straight at Alex.

Both Charlie and Kenneret hit him from behind, and he fell hard on the stairs, hearing the arrows strike the books behind him—*thunk-thunk-thunk*—and clatter off the railing to fall away to the stone floor below.

Charlie pulled him and his sister to their feet. "The marked books are still after you, Alex," he said.

"Yeah, I noticed," Alex shot back.

"You all right?" Franciss asked as she climbed a few steps to reach them, her eye on the passage that had produced the arrows.

Miss Bug pointed with a bony finger. "Archery books down there."

Jeffen was bringing up the rear, five steps below them. "Lion!" he panted. "Still coming!"

Alex looked up. They had two levels to go to reach the fifth floor. Every book in the library was trembling; the cavernous main room was filled with the noise of pages rustling, books bumping on the shelves, the huffs of the lion coming up the stairs after them . . .

. . . and the ringing clash of a hammer striking sparks off a heavy anvil.

"Blacksmithing books down that way, too," Miss Bug piped up.

"Run!" Jeffen yelled.

Alex almost tripped as he raced up the stairs, with Charlie and Kenneret on his heels; from behind came the sound of hot metal hissing with steam; a quick glance back showed him Jeffen—*not* panicking— fighting off a blacksmith's hammer, a whirling anvil, and two rods of iron with coal-bright ends that glowed orange in the dim light. "I'll hold them off!" he shouted. "Keep going!"

The lion roared again.

The roar was answered by a brilliant flash of light from a passage above them on the fourth level, followed by a thundering *boom* that shook the entire library, and an eruption of sooty, black smoke.

Alex knew what it was—the blackpowder explosions book had finally broken out of its barricaded room.

A second blackpowder blast hit, sending flaming books whizzing out into the main area and arcing past them like shooting stars to land on the floor, far below. Alex, Charlie, and Kenneret raced up three more steps to the third-floor balcony with soot and sparks billowing around them.

Fire, Alex realized. In *his* library!

"Come on!" Kenneret yelled back to Franciss and Miss Bug, who had only made it halfway up from the second floor.

There was a third *boom*, and the balcony shuddered under their feet. Alex watched, horrified, as the shock wave of the blast hit the circular stairway leading up to the next floor, and it started unwinding from around its central pole, pieces of carved balcony curling away, the steps rattling apart. Alex threw himself to the balcony floor, scooted to its edge, and shouted down at Franciss and Miss Bug, "Get off the stairs!"

In response, Franciss gave a quick glance upward, saw the stairway unwinding toward her—she grabbed

Miss Bug and leaped for the second-floor balcony, five feet down. "Jeffen!" she shouted, and, below them, he dropped his sword, turned, and grabbed the edge of the balcony as the stairs peeled away, taking the lion with them.

"We're all right!" came Jeffen's choked voice from below.

Alex got to his feet, looking up. Flaming flakes of pages rained down, and billows of soot choked the air.

"We have to keep going." Kenneret was at his side. Her hair was falling out of its braids, and she had a smudge of soot over her cheek, but she looked determined, and every inch a queen.

"Can't," Charlie said, pointing. "No stairs."

"There's another way up." Alex coughed as a billow of smoke wafted past them. Oh please, let the books not burn up. "Come on!"

The library was rumbling with fright and the echoes of the explosions, and the frustrated roars of the lion. They made their way around the third-tier balcony until they reached an arched doorway that led into a pitch-black hallway.

Alex opened his mouth to call for a light-well when two of his pages, their paper a little singed around the edges, darted through the smoke, bringing what he needed. He felt a sudden affection for the pages, so brave, even while their library was under attack. "Thanks," he said, and taking the light-wells, he led Kenneret and Charlie into the passage.

Hurrying, they went down a set of stairs, along a low-ceilinged stone hallway with no bookshelves in it, to a door that, Alex knew, led to another room that would take them to a vertical tunnel that would lead them to the fifth floor.

Alex put his hand on the door's latch, ready to fling it open, then froze. "Wait," he whispered.

From inside the room came the sound of a deep, echoing moan. A puff of greenish dust leaked from the crack under the door.

Oh, blast it.

Holding his breath, Alex carefully lifted his hand from the latch, wiped it on his coat, and backed away.

"What is it?" Charlie whispered.

As an answer, Alex grabbed his arm, and Kenneret's hand, and dragged them halfway down the hall, where he stopped and gasped for breath. "Poisons," he told them. "A room full of books about poisons."

"Is there another way?" Kenneret asked.

Alex nodded. "Come on."

They backtracked until they came to another passage made narrow because the shelves that lined it were filled with books as big as boulders, and about as heavy. "Dictionaries," Alex whispered as they stood in the doorway, looking down the dim passage. He pointed at a door at the other end. "That's where we're going. Be very quiet. We can try to sneak through." He held up the light-well and pointed. "You two go first."

On silent feet, Kenneret led the way into the passage, followed by Charlie.

Alex stepped into the passage. He had barely any warning before the dictionaries attacked.

25

Alex heard a low *thump*. As he was turning to see what it was, he caught a glimpse of the Lost Books symbol edged with flames flying toward him, and one of the dictionaries slammed into him, knocking him off his feet. It was like getting hit by a boulder. The light-well had fallen from his hand; everything was dark. He was facedown on the stone floor, and he couldn't even catch his breath, when another heavy book landed on his back, and another. In the thick blackness, he felt the stone floor, cold and hard under his cheek, and the weight on him, so heavy that he couldn't get any air into his lungs—the dictionaries were trying to suffocate him.

"Oh no you don't!" he heard Charlie shout, and the weight lessened, and then he felt Charlie's hands close around his wrists, and he was dragged along the length of the hall. There was another *thud*, and a weight landed on him again, and the last wisp of air leaked out of his lungs.

"Heave it off!" Kenneret panted.

They shoved the books away, and with the last of his strength Alex scrambled to his knees, gasping for breath. Kenneret pushed him to his feet and through the door at the end of the hallway—she was holding the light-well—and then they were through, and Charlie was slamming the door behind them.

The three of them stood there, panting, staring at each other. A few pages gathered at Alex's shoulder, trembling with fear.

"Thanks." Alex felt bruised from head to foot, as if he'd been picked up by the hand of a giant and *squeezed*.

"You're very welcome," Kenneret replied, handing him the light-well, and to his surprise, she gave him half a smile.

"Now what?" Charlie asked. His eyes gleamed in the dim light.

Alex tried to think of what his pa would do at a moment like this, or what advice he would give, and all of a sudden he missed his father desperately. But the Swift wasn't here, and neither was the Family. "We have to keep going," Alex said raggedly. His ribs creaked as he raised the light-well and pointed up. "That way."

They were in a vertical tunnel with an iron ladder bolted into its smooth stone wall, leading up into murky darkness.

"I'll go first this time," Charlie declared, and started climbing.

Alex handed the light-well to his pages and followed, the rungs of the ladder gritty with rust under his fingers, and then came Kenneret. The tunnel was damp and cold, and the clanking sound of their feet on the metal ladder echoed in creepy ways. They climbed without speaking for a few minutes, until Charlie stopped. Alex looked at his friend's boots, just over his head, and then up at his face. Kenneret's face was a blurred oval in the darkness below him.

"I think this is it," Charlie whispered.

Alex nodded. His bones aching, he went up a few more rungs of the ladder to a low doorway only a foot high. Charlie had already wriggled through it. Alex ducked his head and followed, then creaked to his feet. A moment later, Kenneret stood beside him.

They were at a crossroads, a square room with a

closed door in each wall. Stepping closer to each other, they put their heads together.

"Which door is it?" Kenneret whispered.

"I don't know," Alex answered. "I've looked in here before, but all four doors were locked, and I didn't have the keys. But somebody who's read the Keys Treatise could open them."

"So he could be behind any one of them," Charlie said.

"Let's be sure they're actually locked first," Kenneret said, and stepped toward one of the doors.

"I'll check this one," Charlie said, and went to one of the others.

They both put their hands on the doorknobs at the same time, and found that the doors were locked. With her hand resting on the knob, Kenneret turned and shook her head, and Charlie bent to try peering through the keyhole.

At the same instant, both doors opened with a *whoosh*, Kenneret and Charlie were each sucked into the rooms beyond, and the doors slammed shut behind them with a resounding crash.

In one bound, Alex was at Kenneret's door with his ear pressed against the wood, trying to make out sounds from within. "Kennie!" he shouted. "Are you all right?"

"Yes!" came the faint sound of her voice. "He's not in here!"

From Charlie's door came the sound of pounding—he was already trying to get out.

Then, from behind him, Alex heard the rattle of a key in a lock, and the creaking sound of a door swinging open on unoiled hinges.

He whirled around to face it, knowing what he was going to see.

Lord Patch stood in the arched doorway, slipping a small, square book back into his coat pocket. The Keys Treatise, Alex felt sure. In his other hand, Patch held a length of yellowed paper with ragged edges, half unrolled. The Scroll of Kings. As always, Patch was meticulously dressed in yellow silk and pearls. He was not wearing a sword. His bald head gleamed in the light that emanated from the room behind him. That room was lined with intricately carved bookshelves, polished to a high shine. Every book displayed on the shelves was a treasure—bound in richest leather, titles stamped in gold, written on the finest paper.

Every single one of them was marked with the symbol of the Lost Books.

The symbols were outlined in flames, and they pulsed with power, burning through the covers of the books they marked. Alex could feel the animosity coming off them in waves, all directed at one person—him.

"I'm a librarian," he tried to tell the books.

But Patch was already shaking his head. "You have no idea what you are, do you?" And then he said something completely unexpected. "Show me your left wrist."

"What about it?" Alex said, not moving to obey. He could still hear Charlie banging on his door; Kenneret was silent behind hers—he knew she was listening.

"You are marked," Patch said smoothly. "And you do not know what that means. Every book in this room wants to take its vengeance on you."

"Because you sent them after me," Alex retorted.

Patch was shaking his head, so annoyingly calm. "No. I had nothing to do with that part of it. Well, yes, I woke the Lost Books with my searching, but I did not direct their attacks. All of the Lost Books hate and fear you because of what you are." He patted his coat pocket and held up the half-read scroll. "They sent the marked books after you, and only you. Why is that?"

"I don't know," Alex bit out. His right hand rested on the pommel of his sword. He was ready to fight, if he had to.

"Well, *I* know," Patch said, his voice almost conversational. "You should have listened to me, boy. I tried to warn you. I'm afraid you only have yourself to blame for this." Without taking his eyes off of Alex, he leaned back into the room and took a book from a shelf.

Alex tensed, ready to draw his sword.

With a quick glance, Patch checked the title of the book he'd taken. "Ah, yes. I think this one will do nicely."

And without another word, he tossed the book at Alex.

Slowly it tumbled, end over end, its pages flapping. The symbol on its cover burst into flames. As he felt the book try to force him to start reading, Alex closed his eyes and moved to step out of its way. And then he heard the sleek, steel sound of swords being drawn.

At the same moment, he opened his eyes and snatched his own weapon from its sheath.

Five feet away, four swords hung in the air. One huge, heavy broadsword. One rapier with a needlelike tip. One cutlass with a curve of sharpened blade. And one light, narrow sword like the one he held.

Light glinted from their wickedly sharp edges.

The book hung in the air behind them. The symbol on its cover pulsed. Its pages turned. It would direct this fight.

Alex blocked the sound of Charlie hurling himself at his door, and Kenneret shouting at her uncle to let her out. He ignored Patch leaning almost casually in the doorway, watching. The ache of his bruised ribs faded away. He didn't think of his pa, or consider what advice he would give.

There was no time for thinking, only reacting.

His vision narrowed, focused, until it was just him and the swords.

The broadsword was the first to move, a sweeping blow aimed at Alex's neck, meant to lop his head off, but Alex had already ducked. Then he blocked the rapier's first thrust, and jumped and rolled out of the way as the cutlass tried to cut off his legs at the knees. As he scrambled to his feet, he saw the broadsword cartwheeling around behind him; he blocked a flurry of attacks from the rapier, and felt the sharp edge of the light sword cut a burning line along his ribs.

Panting, he backed away, turning to put the broadsword in front of him again, keeping his blade up, feeling blood seeping into his shirt, under his coat.

The sword that had cut him flicked a drop of blood from its edge, almost as if it was taunting him.

Then the cutlass took up a stance that he recognized. He was moving to block its attack even before it started—at the same time, the broadsword barreled in, and he sidestepped it easily. He parried a flickering attack from the rapier. And as he blocked another obvious swipe from the cutlass, he checked the cover of the book that was directing the fight.

Seeing its title, Alex gasped out a laugh. Of *course*. The book was *The Sword Practicum*, and it was the most basic book on sword fighting. Not only had Alex read it, he had it practically memorized. It meant that he knew what the swords were going to do before they did it.

But there were four of them, and only one of him, and he could feel the blood oozing from the cut over his ribs. He had to end this fight fast, or it would end him.

The rapier attacked next, darting in, trying to nick his arm with its sharp tip. He blocked it with a chopping motion that sent the blade to the floor. Before it could flash up into the air again, he put his foot on it, holding it down. One down, three to go.

"Oh, *very* nicely done," said Patch from his doorway.

A moment of distraction. Alex focused again and realized that he'd lost track of the cutlass. He swung around, keeping the rapier trapped under his foot, in time to see the cutlass sweeping another low blow at his knees. He hurled himself out of the way, but too late—the tip of the blade ripped a gash in the side of his leg. The pain of it made him gasp, and he staggered to his feet, then whirled and brought his sword up again.

Broadsword next—right?

No, light sword. He batted its attack aside, and then he made a mistake. Turning to confront the broadsword, he realized that he'd lost track of the rapier.

A second later it attacked from behind, and he felt the slick, icy feeling of the rapier's tip sliding between his ribs, seeking his heart.

With a yell, he wrenched himself away, then tried to bring his sword up. His own blood was spattered on the floor around him. The pain of the rapier's strike slammed into him. His breath came in ragged gasps.

And then Lord Patch stepped out of his doorway, strode across the room, seized the *Sword Practicum* book, and snapped it shut. "That should do it," he said.

All four blades fell to the floor with a clatter.

Three of them were stained with Alex's blood.

Kenneret watched the fight through the keyhole. She couldn't see much more than light glinting
on sword blades. She heard the clash of steel on steel,
and then more fighting, and she heard Alex yell, then
gasp in pain.

"Oh, no," she whispered.

She gripped the doorknob until her knuckles
turned white. And suddenly, the knob turned and the
door opened, spilling her out into the room.

Quickly she got to her feet, seeing four swords
lying on the floor; blood was spattered around them.
Charlie's door had opened too. He sprawled on the

floor, then rose to a crouch, eyeing the swords, ready to grab one of them and fight.

Alex stood leaning on his own sword, panting, dripping with blood from at least two wounds, his head lowered and a swatch of blond hair hanging down in front of his eyes.

Her uncle stood in the doorway opposite them, framed by books, bathed in candlelight. He held up a scroll of paper. He looked calm, smooth, regal. "You know what this is, my dear."

She nodded. "The Scroll of Kings."

He smiled his toothless smile. "And now I shall use it. Kneel!" He raised the scroll and pointed at her. "Bow to me!"

Two steps away, Alex wavered and fell to his knees.

Her uncle gave a triumphant sneer.

"That was blood loss," Alex snapped, "not the Scroll." He put a bloody hand on the floor to steady himself. "Kennie," he panted, his face as white as paper. "Don't burn it unless you absolutely have to."

Her uncle was gazing at her, a faint frown line gathering on his forehead. "Bow down!" he ordered again, and pointed the Scroll at her.

It had no effect. She straightened, gathering her queenliness around her.

Patch reached back, pulled a marked book off the

shelf of the room behind him, and hurled it at her. It landed with a thud on the floor at her feet. Just a book. No threat to someone who wasn't a librarian.

Calmly she stepped around it. Nearby, Charlie slowly rose to a stand. "What do you think the Scroll is for, Uncle Patch?" she said softly.

"It gives me power," he answered. "The power to rule."

"What does that even mean?" Charlie asked.

"It means being king," he said grandly. "As I was meant to be. I will command. I will be obeyed. I will destroy the Greylings to the north, freeing up the Swift and his soldiers to expand the borders of the kingdom. We will increase our trade revenue. Sixty years ago we were one of the greatest kingdoms in the world, and we have declined into a backwards land populated by dirt-grubbing farmers. I have the strength and vision that you lack, Kenneret, and the power to rule will enable me to make my vision a reality."

"I don't think that's what it says in the Scroll," she said, pointing at it. "Does it?"

She heard Alex give a weary laugh. "He hasn't had time to read it all yet."

"It was written by a good king," Kenneret went on. "One who knew that ruling does not mean forcing obedience." She took a measured step closer to him. "I'll tell you what a queen does, Uncle Patch; I'll tell you how a good king rules," she said steadily. "Ruling does not mean dominating. It means making difficult decisions. It means working hard, all the time, late into every night. It means listening to the farmers' guild, and the trade guild, and explaining to them why paying taxes is a good thing. It means . . ." She faltered. "It means . . ."

"The royal *we*," she heard Alex say faintly.

"Yes," she said with a nod. "I don't speak for myself. I speak for the land, and the people. I put them ahead of myself, *always*."

"It's the opposite of dominating, really," Charlie said, with the clear-sighted intelligence she'd started to expect from him.

"That's right," Kenneret said. She lifted her chin and gazed at her uncle, who stared back at her, his mouth open a little. "I am queen," she said simply. "*We* are queen. And as long as we are alive, Uncle, you will never rule this kingdom."

"As long as you are alive?" he said, snapping to attention again. In one graceful move, he bent, grabbed the short sword from the floor, and was on his feet again, sighting down the blade. "I don't need any scroll for this."

Quickly she surveyed the swords that were left on the floor. Broadsword—too heavy. Cutlass—too limited.

Deciding, she bent and seized the rapier, which had Alex's blood crusting at its tip. Leaping to her feet, her skirts swirling around her, she raised the rapier just as her uncle lunged toward her, his sword aimed at her heart.

Ignoring Charlie's yell of warning, and Alex's dismayed gasp, she focused all of her attention on the blade coming toward her. Smoothly, with the ease of long practice, she parried the short sword and launched her own attack, the tip of her rapier opening a gash along the yellow silk of her uncle's sleeve. He flinched away, then raised his sword again. "You've been—" He panted. "You've been studying the sword?"

"Yes, Uncle Patch," she said softly, without taking her eyes from his. "For years. I'm very good."

"Good?" His usually calm face distorted into a snarl. "You are no threat to me—you are nothing more than a little girl!" And he came at her again, in a rush, his sword swinging wildly.

"A girl," she answered calmly, leaning away and letting one of his swings flail past her nose, "who had sense enough to know that as queen, I would need to learn"—she parried his blade and flicked the wickedly sharp tip of the rapier against his sword hand—"how to fight."

His hand streaming blood, he dropped his sword,

which fell to the floor with a clatter.

"And how to win," she added, and brought the rapier up and held it to her uncle's throat.

At the same moment, she heard a rush of footsteps from behind the room's fourth door.

In here, sir! she heard—the voice of the Family soldier Jeffen. Then a jingle of keys at the lock. "Charlie!" she ordered. A second later, her brother was at her side. "Take this." She handed him the rapier and stepped back. No sense in revealing her skill with the sword, since she'd been keeping it a secret for so long. Charlie nodded, understanding, and pointed the rapier at their uncle, who was staring at her, blood dripping from his hand and staining his coat sleeve.

She saw Alex trying to struggle to his feet. He caught her eye. "I can't let him see me like this," he gasped.

With a nod, she rushed to his side and grabbed his elbow, hauling him up.

The door burst open, and the Swift strode into the room.

27

Alex saw his father survey the room in one eagle-like glance, taking in Lord Patch with Charlie holding the rapier at his throat; the queen, safe; the two blood-ied swords on the floor. The dark eyes narrowed as they fell on Alex.

"Jeffen, Franciss," the Swift ordered, pointing toward Patch without taking his eyes from Alex. The two Family soldiers, sleek and deadly in their black uniforms, swarmed into the room and grabbed the queen's uncle, while Charlie stepped back and lowered the rapier. The steward was there, too, with the ring of keys that she'd used to open the door. They all smelled faintly of smoke.

Charlie stared at the Swift, his eyes wide and full of hero worship.

The Swift nodded to the queen, who was still at Alex's side. Holding him up, he had to admit. His head was spinning from blood loss and exhaustion, and every inch of him hurt.

"Just prop me against the wall," he muttered to Kenneret, "and step aside. There's going to be shouting."

"Shut up, Alex," she whispered back.

The Swift had his hands on his hips. His keen eyes examined Alex from head to foot. "You all right, son?"

Alex couldn't meet his gaze. "Just fine, obviously."

"Good." And then his pa crossed the space between them, grabbed Alex, and swept him into a hug.

"Ow, Pa," Alex gasped. "Ribs."

"Idiot," his father growled, and then Alex felt him kiss the top of his head, and then his big hands were setting him back against the wall, and he'd turned and started issuing orders, flinging a question at the steward, asking the queen where they should imprison Lord Patch, saying that the fire in the library was under control.

Charlie sidled closer. "Good thing I've got the thinking-mitten," he heard Charlie say, and then he felt the other boy use it to try to stop the bleeding from the rapier wound.

Alex's head was floating very far above the rest of his body. He felt his knees shaking, and then he slid to the floor and everything went black.

He woke up not much later, bandaged, in a bedroom draped in black velvet and encrusted with tarnished gold. A few of his pages hovered worriedly near his pillow. Sitting up in the bed, he felt a deep ache in his bones, and a sharper pain where the rapier had gone in. But his head was clear. Sort of. Carefully he swung his legs out of the bed.

"Oh, you're awake, are you?" Charlie asked, getting up from a nearby chair.

Alex gave him his nastiest glare, which was returned with a typically Charlie grin. "I have to talk to your sister," Alex said. He was wearing his own trousers over the bandage on his leg, and a clean shirt over the bandages on his chest. Charlie's shirt, judging by how big it was on him.

"She's busy," Charlie said. "Now, the doctor left you this medicine." He crossed to a table, where he poured something into a glass, which he brought to Alex.

Alex examined the liquid, then sniffed it. "I'm not drinking this."

"Yes you are," Charlie said, and stood over him

with arms folded until he'd gulped half of it down.

"So . . ." Charlie began.

Alex interrupted him with a brisk "No." He knew what his friend wanted to talk about.

Ignoring his protest, Charlie asked, "The Swift is your father?"

"What do you think?" Alex said sharply. "You were there when he called me his son, weren't you?"

"Yes, but I can't help but notice," Charlie said cheerfully, "you look nothing like him. He's got that rich skin color of the old nobility, and you're as pale as paper." He looked Alex over. "Even paler than usual, really."

"Oh, you noticed that, did you?" Alex asked, letting acid drip from his words. Then he sighed. "It's a long story, Charlie, and I'm not going to tell it to you now."

"All right," Charlie said, unfazed. "He's amazing, isn't he?"

"Yes," Alex agreed. "He is." He didn't want what his pa wanted, but it didn't mean he loved his pa any less.

"Welp, you'd better drink the rest of the medicine," Charlie said, and held up the glass.

After he'd forced the rest of it down, Alex got to his feet. Which were bare. "Where are my shoes?" he asked, looking around.

"You're supposed to stay in bed," Charlie protested.

"I told you," Alex said, fixing on the bedroom door. "I have to talk to the queen."

Ignoring Charlie's protests, he started toward the door, only wobbling a little bit. He had to make sure she hadn't burned the Scroll or the Keys Treatise, and he had to be sure the fire in the library was well and truly out, and he had to start going through the books to find out what had been burned, and what could be salvaged, and . . . .

Opening the door, he walked right into Kenneret, who had been about to come into the room. Behind her loomed the Swift, and three of the Family, and the steward with her pinched, disapproving mouth.

Alex staggered back, then braced himself against the door frame. "Your Majesty," he began. "You haven't—"

"Alex," she interrupted. "What are you doing out of bed?"

"Sorry, Kennie," Charlie put in. "He said he had to talk to you."

"We are sure that he thinks he does," she said.

"Since you're up, Alexandren," the Swift said in the tone he used when giving orders, "you can get properly dressed and ready to leave."

"I'm not leaving," Alex told him.

His pa's thick eyebrows lowered. One of them was

bisected by an old scar that ran over his forehead and into his hairline. "You are going back home to resume your training."

"No I'm not," Alex insisted. His head was starting to feel funny again. "I'm staying here. I'm a librarian. It's not—"

Kenneret raised her hand, interrupting him, and he fell silent. She was still bedraggled from their pursuit of Lord Patch, smudged with dust and soot, with a smear of his own blood down her right sleeve, her hair straggling out of its braids, and she looked more queenly than he'd ever seen her. "Alex," she said calmly, and pointed. "Bed. Now."

With a sigh, Alex turned and trudged back to the bed.

"How did you do that, Your Majesty?" he heard his father ask.

"Do what?" Kenneret responded.

His pa blew out a frustrated breath. "Get him to do what he's told."

"We are the queen," was Kenneret's simple answer. She *was*.

And he was a librarian. Why couldn't his pa see that? Alex flopped down on the bed. The medicine they'd given him must've had a sleeping draft in it. His eyelids felt so heavy. "Kennie," he murmured. "Don't burn the Scroll, all right?" He had to tell her what he'd realized while she'd been telling Lord Patch what being queen *really* meant. The Lost Books. He'd been right about them all along—yes, they hated him, but they were *not* evil. They all had the *self* of their writer trapped in them. They were alive. He was a librarian, and it wasn't his job to lock them up, or destroy them, or kill them.

He had to find all of the Lost Books and figure out how to set them free.

He heard footsteps cross the room and then felt her warm breath on his cheek as she bent to whisper in his ear. "Don't worry, Alex. I'm not going to burn any books. Go to sleep."

And so he did.

Somehow Kenneret had gotten his pa to go back to the fortress and the Family without him.

Well, not *somehow*. She must have done that *queen* thing. She'd gotten really good at it.

Things with his pa weren't settled yet—they weren't even close to being settled—and part of him wished he *could* go back to the fortress and be the Family's little brother, and take up his training again, and be the son his pa really wanted. But he couldn't.

Because he had work to do.

His recovery from the fight with the swords didn't take very long. As soon as he was up, he went to find Kenneret in her office, where she had piles of papers on her polished desk, with secretaries bustling in and out carrying letters and files. Her steward was there, too, giving Alex a gimlet-eyed look as he came in.

The queen signed something, gave it to a secretary, and nodded at Alex. "Dorriss, a chair for the librarian, please."

"I'm fine," Alex said impatiently. "I just want the keys to the library back." Someone—the steward, he guessed—had taken them while he'd been recovering.

One of the secretaries placed a chair before her desk.

With a huff of impatience, he sat. "I don't have time for this," he complained. "The books have to be settled. I need to be sure the Lost Books are safe, and start repairing the damage from the fire. Among other things."

With extremely exasperating calm, Kennie folded her hands and rested them on a stack of papers on her desk. "Alex," she began.

"What." He narrowed his eyes. She was up to something.

"My uncle said something very interesting when I was fighting him. Did you notice?"

"I'd just had several holes poked in me," he said. "I was a little distracted." He shifted on his chair. It had the world's hardest pillow on it. From what he could see, the queen had a fluffy, very comfortable-looking pillow on her own chair.

"I will remind you," she said. "He said that our country was far greater sixty years ago than it is now. Sixty years. An interesting number, don't you think?"

Suddenly, he was paying attention. "That's when the Lost Books were created. The librarians fought them, and then they closed the libraries."

"Yes. For the past sixty years," Kennie said, "this country has been weakening, stagnant. My uncle was right about that. He assumed it meant we need a man like him to be a strong leader. But that's not what we need. For sixty years, nothing has changed. Nothing new has been invented, no new knowledge has been created, no new books have been written. We look inward, we don't ask any questions. For sixty years, Alex, the libraries have been locked."

His heart was pounding. "And they have to stay locked."

"Is that so?" She cocked her head and gave him a keen look. He'd seen it before—she'd had the same focused look on her face when she'd faced down her uncle's sword. "Then I have a question for you, Librarian. What is a book's purpose? What is a book *for*?"

He wasn't sure what she was getting at. "A book is for reading."

She nodded. "Exactly." She smiled. "I am glad we

agree. You will prepare the library to be opened."

"Wait, what?" He got to his feet, ignoring the twinge from the almost-healed rapier wound. "*Opened?* No. Absolutely not."

She stood, her hands on her desk, leaning toward him. On her braided hair, the crown gleamed, and her face was alight with excitement. She was somebody, Alex realized, who didn't need any magical scroll to be a great queen. She had *vision.* "Alex, you idiot," she said quickly. "Books should not be covered with dust in locked-up libraries. They're supposed to be alive and awake and *read.* By *readers.* You should know this! You're a *librarian!*"

He blinked and felt like he'd just had an entire shelf of books dropped on his head.

Because she was right. It wasn't just the Lost Books.

All of the books needed to be free.

Alex and Miss Bug were sitting across from each other at one of the long reading tables in the cavernous main room of the library, going through the cards from the catalog. His pages fluttered around him, ready to go search for books and report back if they found them.

Tiny Miss Bug sat on a pile of four pillows to bring

her up to the level of the table. She peered at a card and set it in the pile they'd set aside for books that were still missing.

The Scroll of Kings and the Keys Treatise were locked in a metal box in the fortified room, along with all the other books that had been marked. They'd be safe there, as long as nobody tried to read them, as Patch had.

The winding staircases that had been destroyed when the blackpowder book had exploded were still damaged. He and Bug were using tall ladders to get from one level to the next. A dusting of soot covered everything. There was a blackened crater on the fourth floor, and the arrows that had been aimed at him still bristled from the books near the stairs on the second level. Hundreds of other books were scattered around the main room. Many shelves of books in the rest of the library had been damaged. It would take years to set it right.

But he was a librarian. That was his job.

And once they had the worst of the mess cleared up, he'd do what the queen ordered. He'd open up the library so the books could be read.

He made a note on a catalog card and passed it across the table to Miss Bug. She blinked at it, wrinkled up her nose, and put it on the *Not Found* pile.

Alex arranged six more cards on the table before him. Then he paused and looked up. Absently he rubbed the ring of letters that encircled his left wrist. The table, he realized, was vibrating.

Miss Bug looked up from her work and met his gaze. Her big eyes blinked behind her thick spectacles.

From overhead came a screeching sound, like something hurtling very fast through the air. A second later, three books, their covers flapping like wings, shot from an arched doorway on the fifth level. Banking, they folded their pages back and plummeted through the big room. Aimed at him.

The Lost Books symbol blazed from the covers of all three books.

Pushing back his chair, Alex dove under the table, then crawled across and grabbed Miss Bug and dragged her under, too.

Thump-thump-thump as all three books hit the tabletop. Catalog cards blew up and then rained down all around them.

Blast it, Alex thought. That was *days* of work.

"Out!" piped Miss Bug, and pointed with a twiglike finger at the library door.

As more books dive-bombed them, he and Bug scrambled from under the table.

They stumbled out into the hallway, slamming the door behind them.

Panting, Alex slid down to sit on the worn carpet

of the hallway floor, leaning on the wall. Miss Bug crouched beside him.

They both eyed the library door. It shuddered under the sound of the three books—or more—battering at it, trying to get out.

"I thought we were done with this," Alex said.

"I *told* you," Miss Bug said, sounding satisfied. "You should hide."

"I hate it when you're cryptic," he said, giving her a narrow-eyed glare. "Can't you just come out and tell me what you know?"

She folded herself into a ball and sat with her chin on her knees, looking like a little fluffy owl. "I'm not a librarian. I don't know as much as you think I do." After a silent moment, her little hands reached out and pushed up the cuff of his shirt, revealing the ring of letters printed around his wrist. "Tell how this happened."

Yes, she was right. It all had to do with the fact that he was marked.

"Tell," Miss Bug prompted.

"All right," Alex agreed. "When I was a kid, I found the key to my pa's library, and I went in and read every book in it." He went on to tell her the rest of the story, how he'd found the Red Codex that smelled of spices and smoke, how it was heavier than the other books. Then he told how the words had crawled out of the

Codex and around his wrist, and how the letters sometimes re-formed into words of warning or advice. As he finished telling, he studied the jumble of letters, dark against his pale skin.

And he remembered something Lord Patch had said to him. *You have no idea what you are, do you?* It was true. "I don't know what I am," he concluded. He studied the letters on his wrist to see if they'd oh-so-helpfully give him some advice. But of course they didn't.

"I do," Miss Bug said. "I know what you are."

"Oh, really," Alex muttered crossly, and pulled down his sleeve again to cover the letters.

"Yes." Miss Bug's little face grew serious, the eyes huge behind the thick lenses of her spectacles. "You're not just *a* librarian." Somehow the words sounded weighty. "You are *the* Librarian."

As she spoke, the bracelet of letters around Alex's wrist itched. He pushed up his sleeve again to see what the letters had to say.

POIEDSOINXLIEIEKSXXWQOINX

"That's not particularly helpful," Alex told them. Then, like spindly-legged ants, the letters crawled over each other, shifted again, and spelled out two words.

THE LIBRARIAN

And it was true.

He was.

≋ Acknowledgments ≋

Thanks to all the librarians. You know who you are. Specifically thanks to the librarians who kindly gave me permission to kill them off in this book (with their names slightly altered): Mary Rumsey, Maeve Clark, Jackie Hockett Biger. And to the memory of Kathryn Farnsworth, storyteller, librarian, and the person who first pointed me toward books.

To the bestest BFFs in the world: Jenn Reese, Deb Coates, and Greg van Eekhout. You guys.

And seriously, without Michelle Edwards this book might not exist. Thanks, pal, for all the long talks and long walks and for urging me to send the "librarian kid book" to my agent. All the pompons and all the woolly hats in this book are for you.

To my friend Luke Reynolds and my intern, Lee Hartley. And to the memory of my dearest Ellie Ditzel.

To my awesome colleagues at Prairie Lights Books, a great bookstore. You should all visit it, especially on Sunday afternoons when I'm working in the kids section downstairs.

To this book's readers. This was the most fun I've ever had writing a book—and I hope you have as much fun reading it.